The Long

The Long Lost Tal
epic fantasy unive
story, whereas Th̶ ̶̶̶̶̶ ̶̶̶̶̶̶ ̶̶̶̶̶̶̶ ̶̶̶̶̶̶ ̶̶̶̶̶̶̶es runs alongside it. To
understand one series, it's in no way necessary to read any other
work, though it's recommended that the books are read in order,
as references are made and reading all books will grant a deeper
understanding of the world in which these tales take place.

Books by Patrick Hall

THE LONG LOST TALES OF THE DRAGONLANDS

THE GUARDIAN BLADES SERIES
Blades in the Dark (October 28, 2013)

THE DRAGON HUNTER SERIES
The Winds of Change (December 9, 2013)

The Long Lost Tales of the Dragonlands

Blades in the Dark

***

Patrick Hall

BLADES IN THE DARK

Copyright © 2013 by Patrick Hall.

Edited by Patrick Hall.
"Dark Trees and a Bleak Sky" cover art by Patrick Hall.
Cover designed by Patrick Hall.
Cover picture taken in Mölndal, Sweden.

A self-published book.
Published independently by Patrick Hall.

www.authorpatrickhall.com
www.facebook.com/patrickhallofficial
www.twitter.com/AuthorPatHall
patrickhallofficial@gmail.com

ISBN-10 (paperback): 1491276495
ISBN-13 (paperback): 978-1491276495
ASIN (The Guardians of Siva): B00G91KZYU
ASIN (Tah Ansenta Mas'plu): B00GLPRYO8
ASIN (Into the Fire): B00GWI2FV6

First paperback edition: October 28, 2013.
First e-book edition (The Guardians of Siva): October 28, 2013.
First e-book edition (Tah Ansenta Mas'plu): November 11, 2013.
First e-book edition (Into the Fire): November 25, 2013.
This second paperback edition: March 17, 2014.

Preface

A story is about to unfold

Blades in the Dark is special to me—especially part one, *The Guardians of Siva*. It is because that part of the trilogy is the first thing I ever finished. It is not the first thing I ever started, though; I started writing my soon-to-be debut novel *The Winds of Change* before it. Nonetheless, the trilogy is special to me, as it is the first book I ever released as a professional author, which is a huge thing.

I wrote the trilogy because I wanted a short story to sell to a website to get renown and hopefully a publisher. Realizing it was moronic trying to sell part one of a trilogy to a website that wanted short stories and that Amazon has the amazing CreateSpace and Kindle Direct Publishing services, I put the trilogy on the shelf to focus on my novel.

I think I did the right thing. The Winds of Change quickly turned into my defining piece of work. Where did that leave Blades in the Dark? Editing my novel took me longer than I planned, so I thought I'd finish Blades in the Dark and publish it first. That way, the hints about the novel's plot didn't appear so pointless and I could at least try to build hype for my first major work.

Either way, the Blades in the Dark trilogy—a third of it at least—is my first completed manuscript. It is the first work I ever published, which in writing moment has yet to occur. It feels monumental; this book is a significant milestone in my career, and in my life.

In some ways, Blades in the Dark could be considered my first novel. While individually the parts are defined as novelettes (not actually short stories, but I digress), together they reach the word count of roughly forty-five thousand. So per certain definitions, they are a novel.

Not only is Blades in the Dark my first completed work—

writing and editing—and my first publication, but it is also my very first novel. With this under my belt, I am a true and (self-)published author and novelist. At last, I have set off on the greatest journey of my life.

Now comes your turn, dear reader, to partake in the story about to unfold. The magical Dragonlands hold many tales, and a new one is just getting started...

Author Patrick Hall

Words for distance

The following is a list of words used for distance in the book. Note that when the bigger ones—like leap, tileap, or tenleap—are used, the distance referenced is often a rough value. Non-metric readers can round off (i.e. one leap equals one meter, but can be rounded off to one yard).

A *pac* equals a centimeter, circa 0.4 inches.

A *tapac* equals a decimeter, circa four inches.

A *pace* equals half a meter, circa half of a yard.

A *leap* equals a meter, circa 1.1 yards.

A *tileap* equals a kilometer, circa 0.62 American miles.

A *tenleap* equals ten kilometers, circa 6.2 American miles.

VIII

SUMMER FADES TO FALL

Like a flower that withers as summer turns to fall.
Like a flower that dies as fall turns to winter.
A beautiful, white mat, covering the hidden death beneath.
Shall spring ever come again?
Shall the summer sun warm the air I breathe again?
If the sun won't rise, how could it?
The sun has set for the last time.
All that remains is darkness.
Cold, cold darkness.
All that remains is death.
Cold, cold death.
As I try to cling on to the memory of warmth,
All I can feel around me is cold.
The memory of summer is forever tainted by winter's cold.

***

For my beloved grandmother, Kerstin Hallgren.
May 9, 1936 – February 13, 2013
May you forever rest in peace,
and may your wings carry you to Evengarden.

Acknowledgements

For helping me by giving me feedback and making Blades in the Dark what it is now, many thanks to my brother Rikard "Rick" Hallgren and my friend Carl Johansson. The hugest of thank-you's to the good people at Amazon for their amazing CreateSpace and Kindle Direct Publishing services, as they make publishing not only possible, but easy for new authors like me.

Blades
in
the
Dark

PROLOGUE

The man pulled his hands across his smooth face, as he let out a heavy sigh. He continued, with his hands, up through his hair, and opened his eyes to meet a lovely sight.

"Good morning, husband," the naked woman sitting atop him said with a gentle smile.

"Ain't such a thing as a good morning, darling Anne," the husband said. He watched her lovely face and flowing, dark hair, and let his hands wander up her sides to her breasts. "Now I have to get up and leave this."

With a cute giggle, she leaned in and kissed him. "Sorry, I didn't mean to be a tease."

As she got off him and moved to the wardrobe to pick out this day's wear, he sat up to watch her. He did so until her skin was concealed beneath a dress.

"You ain't nothing but a tease, huh?" he asked.

She smiled as she left the room. It took a while for him to gather his thoughts to a state where he could get up and get dressed. He grabbed his sword—his long-trusted guardian—and headed downstairs.

When he got there, breakfast was already served. His wife wasn't alone by the table; another lovely angel was there, no more than six years old. He stood in the kitchen's doorway, viewing them quietly. They were remarkably alike; his young daughter was her mother's reflection.

When the girl spotted him, she rushed off of her chair, to him. She instantly embraced him in a hug. "Father!"

"Hey, angel," he said, as he watched his wife look on with a tight smile. "Ain't you supposed to finish breakfast? I hear you and mom will buy a new toy today."

"I am done, I am done, I am done!" the little girl said. She rushed to her mother instead, and tugged at the dress. "Can

1

we, can we, can we!? Please!"

"Sure, Tilda," Anne said. "If your father doesn't mind eating alone."

"Nah, I don't mind," the father said.

"Thank you, father," Tilda said.

After getting a goodbye kiss on the cheek from each of the ladies, the man sat down to eat. He placed his sword on the table, something his wife never allowed him to do. He loved her, but she didn't understand. The sword was more than a sword. It had been with him from the very beginning.

He had left the Imperial Legion for her, but he could never truly leave. Becoming a soldier meant being one for the rest of his life. He had seen so much death, he did not think he would ever see anything worse.

Lost in thoughts and ladling porridge into a bowl, something caught his attention. A shadow flew past the kitchen window. He barely had enough time to turn his head.

"What the—"

Crash! The front door, just outside the kitchen's doorway, was bashed open with such force it slammed shut again, but first a couple men stormed in. The husband didn't recognize them; they were strangers, clothed in dark clothing covering their bodies and carrying swords.

They charged toward him. He hurled his bowl of porridge at one of them, splashing the hot contents onto his face. He grasped the sword atop the table and swung it in a sideways arc toward the other stranger.

The sword made contact, slicing apart the stranger by his chest. Blood splashed out all over the clean kitchen. Before the other stranger had time to remove the hot porridge from his face, the husband ran the sword into his heart.

The husband took a step back, holding the bloody sword. He viewed the death he caused. It was a while since he had killed, but the numbness to it that could only be created by war was still there. Looking at all the red, he felt nothing at all—exhilaration, shock, shame, pride... nothing.

He shrugged off the callousness, a mantle of worry wrapping itself around him instead; his wife and daughter were outside somewhere.

He headed through the kitchen, to the entry hall, paying little attention to his surrounds; his mind raced too quickly. He grabbed the doorknob of the front door, but froze looking out of the little window on the door.

The people of the tiny village where he lived were gathered in the courtyard outside his home. Plenty more dark-clothed strangers walked around them, like guards. Every so often, they charged half a leap toward the crowd to scare them, to which the people staggered away.

The man swept his gaze across the crowd, picking out his wife and daughter. He found them quickly, hunkered down in the outskirts of the group. Anne was holding on to Tilda, as they both cried. The man's heart was tied into a knot.

He continued looking through the small window, counting the strangers. There were at least a dozen, too many for him to handle on his own.

Yet another man announced his presence. He entered the courtyard surrounded by houses and headed to the huddled masses. He wore dark robes with a hood over his face.

As he neared the people, the strangers forced them aside, so a clear path was created. The new figure moved through this corridor, and as he reached the center of the crowd, he raised his arms. The villagers backed away, creating a clear area in the center of the group when he did this.

"Ladies!" the hooded man called out. With a movement of his hand, the ground beneath him rose to create a platform of rock. "Gentlemen!"

Mumbles spread through the crowd. What had they seen? Magic? The husband watching through the window was just as amazed; he was dazzled.

"You've lived safe lives here in Tauni, encircled by mountains. Though the Black Hand has terrorized others here in eastern Cyra, you have gone unscathed. You've been lucky. You're about to be even luckier. I am Angus Kritz. I am doing the work of the True God."

The hooded man—Angus Kritz—moved his hand, raising the ground again, creating a bed of rock. He moved to it and let his fingers graze against it.

"Bring me the first one," he said, so it was barely audible for the man looking on through the window in the door.

The silent strangers started moving around their captives, scrutinizing them with concealed gazes. One stepped toward the crowd, and grabbed hold of Tilda.

The father bashed his hand to the door. "No! Not her!"

Anne refused to let go of her daughter. She screamed and fought, but the stranger dragged both onto the platform and to Kritz. There, he managed to free Anne's grasp around her daughter, and pushed her away.

"This one," the stranger said, with a tight grip of the girl.

Angus Kritz watched him for a few seconds, and nodded. "That one."

As Kritz grabbed hold of the feisty girl and threw her onto the altar, the stranger restrained Anne. The other strangers moved onto the platform, and brought out candles. They lit them with cold, blue flames in a circle around the altar.

Kritz moved a hand over Tilda, and she instantly became still, as if paralyzed. "You are about to witness the holiest of acts," he mumbled.

He raised his arms and mumbled incoherently. The man watching from behind the door felt the power of the words, even from where he stood. He could see their power, as the air was darkened and wind swooshed around.

The man could not watch it. He could not wrap his head around what was going on. Not long ago, he had enjoyed the company of his family. Now, his daughter was lying on some altar, with this hooded figure Angus Kritz doing Gods know what to her.

The man moved to the window again. He had to see what was going on. Kritz still stood above the girl, who was paralyzed. He reached inside his robes, and clutched something. The father watched in horror as he took out a dagger.

"This is to fight injustice," Kritz said, raising the dagger. "The tyranny will soon be over."

"Nooo!" the father screamed, bursting out of the door with his sword ready.

Everyone's attention turned to him, and Kritz even halted in his action, stopping the dagger mere pacs from the crying girl's belly.

The father ran toward them. He saw red; Kritz had to die. He had to rescue his family. One of the strangers came for him, but was stopped by a sword to the throat. Another one was stopped by a slash against his stomach.

Something blunt smashed him in his back, forcing him to his knees. He was enclosed by the strangers, and then they beat him. He could hear someone shout—a woman—but he could not make it out. The punches left him dazed.

He looked up, but everything was blurry. He could barely make out Kritz, his wife, his daughter. All he saw were blurry shapes and movements. All he heard were the inaudible screams of two women, one adult and one child.

After that followed the color red, more screams, and more red. He could not see it, but he knew what was happening. He forced his vision to focus; he had to see, even if he could not stand the sight of it.

As his vision became clear, his eyes met something different. He saw a humanoid creature, with skin black as death. It had distinct, chiseled features. It was demonic. It was the worst thing he had ever seen in his whole life.

In its presence, his daughter was gone; she had vanished. The father swallowed the tears as he breathed unsteadily.

Black blood spattered out of the demons stomach, but he could not see what had caused it. Then, after no more than a moment, a man became visible behind it, holding a sword pierced through it. He wore black leather armor, reinforced with plates of another kind of material. Over that, he wore a dark-gray cloak.

He pushed the demon off of his sword, letting it fall to the ground, and then ran a hand through his thick, blood-filled beard. He looked across the crowd, taking in the sight of the strangers. A second later, these masked strangers were run through, too, and more warriors appeared from thin air.

The first of these invisible warriors turned to Angus Kritz and the masked warrior holding Anne. He headed for them with his blood-stained sword ready.

"So, the time is not yet ready," Kritz said. "But believe me, one day soon, the time of reckoning will be upon us. Those who stand with the false gods will pay for their ignorance."

He raised his arms, sending out a burst of potent magic. Everyone on the platform—the warrior, the stranger, Anne— was knocked down. Kritz seized Anne and dragged her away as she screamed and struggled.

The husband staggered to his feet. "Anne!" He fell down, and felt tears roll down his cheek. "Anne. Tilda."

He sensed a presence above. He looked up, to see the one who had killed the demon. The man held out a hand to him. He didn't take it. He sat down, unable to get up.

"I am Sir Rither Pleagau, a knight of the Guardian Blades of Siva," the man said. "I have chased Kritz for months. I am sorry I could not come sooner."

The husband grabbed hold of Rither and dragged himself up, before pushing him aside and staggering forward, in the direction Kritz and Anne disappeared. He couldn't see them; they were gone. So was his daughter; merely bloody remains were left of her.

"I'll kill you for this! I'll fucking kill you!" he shouted. "I'll carve out your Gods-damned heart! You hear me!? I'll carve out your fucking heart!"

THE GUARDIANS OF SIVA

1

"Are you sure he's in there, Master?"

"Have I ever been wrong, Brother Sizle?"

"I guess you haven't," Brother Sizle answered with his soft and high, yet masculine voice. "What do you think, Brother Manden?"

"I think you oughta shut your damn mouth and listen to Master Pleagau," Brother Manden responded with his deep and rough voice. "And don't call me Manden!"

"Lay off the kid, Brother Emery," a smooth voice said.

Emery Manden snorted. "If I don't, Brother Tryden!?"

"Emery, Gelan, both of you, shut up," Master Pleagau ordered. "He's in there. I know it. We're also going in there. We won't come out until we have that scum with us, so he can be hanged."

"Rither, uhm, I mean Master Pleagau, what if the rumors are true?" Brother Sizle stammered. "What if there really are Maenics in there?"

"I'm sorry, Anthony, but if you are afraid of encountering Maenics, you should consider another profession. Maenics are what we're about; they are why we exist."

Anthony Sizle laughed nervously. "Sorry, I'm just excited. This is my first real mission."

"I recollect my first mission," Gelan Tryden reminisced. "I caught a Maenic summoner, but no Maenics."

"Have you run into Maenics afterward?" Sizle asked.

"Once. Master Pleagau killed it as I stood frozen. They are fearsome creatures."

Silence fell upon the four men. Suddenly, Emery grunted, "I recall my first mission, too. Killed two dozen people."

Sizle swallowed as he looked to Emery's imposing stature. "You killed two dozen people?"

"A bunch of old men." Noticing the look on Sizle's face, he continued. "Don't worry about it, kid. They weren't innocent grandpas."

Rither laughed softly. He was the only person who understood and appreciated Emery Manden in all his blunt glory. The two of them had worked together for a long time. Emery was his friend.

The four of them were knights of the Guardian Blades, an order dedicated to safeguard the mortal plane of existence, Siva, from unholy threats—Maenics.

Their black leather armor was reinforced with cloud iron. Cloud iron was usually white, turning black only after contact with dragon fire. Since dragons were extinct, the armor had to be painted. Dark-gray cloaks covered the armor, but the hoods were hung back. Their swords rested comfortably in bottomless scabbards strapped to their backs.

The men stood in the Cyran wilderness. An ethereal moon lit up the cold and damp night, revealing the trees towering up all around them and the old, weathered fort.

The fort's once protective walls had many gaps and holes. Its once mighty gates had molded and fallen to pieces. While the fort wasn't big, Rither knew it could continue for tileaps underground. The one they were after could be anywhere in those tileaps of tunnels.

Rither pulled up his hood. "Let's head in there. Invaesen aktivaae."

The others also pulled up their hoods and said, "Invaesen aktivaae," and all vanished; they were made invisible by the magic of their cloaks—silk veils. All knights of the Guardian Blades wore silk veils; they had done so for many thousand years.

Now invisible, they headed to the molded-away gates. The inner courtyard was overgrown, with trees, bushes, plants, and grass. Footprints were clearly visible in the high grass; someone had been there recently.

Rither placed a contented grin on his invisible face. "I told you he's here. Let's head inside."

They walked to the gates of the actual fort. Rither pulled open the heavy doors, and gazed into the darkness. Nothing appeared to be there, but the dark frightened him; anything could be hiding in it.

After a few silent moments, they headed in. On their way, Emery cursed and Sizle grunted when they moved into each other; Sizle wasn't a seasoned blade. Shushing them, Rither focused on the hallway. He studied every dark corner, every dark shape.

The corridor stretched ahead a dozen leaps, two doors on each side, and ended in a set of stairs. The four rooms were empty and dark, filled only with debris. Holes in the ceiling let in the beautiful glint of a thousand stars outside.

Rither commanded the others to move on, and they headed down the stairs into a new passageway. They soon took a ninety-degree turn to the right. On their left, a stone railing overlooked a spacious room.

They moved—quietly and invisibly—across the hallway to another set of stairs. It spiraled down and ended up in the spacious room they had seen before.

The room was beautifully crafted, with pillars reaching up in an arc. Intricate patterns were carved into the pillars and walls. It was a beautiful front for the horror they would find below, past the wide opening on the far side of the room.

The atmosphere was stale and moist. It weighed heavy on Rither's shoulders. He also recognized the distinct feeling of magic.

"Stay frosty, brothers," he said. "Anything could be hiding in the darkness."

"How right you are," a voice said from the dark up ahead. "Many things lurk in the dark."

Rither Pleagau drew his sword, hearing his fellow blades do the same. "Who's there!? Show yourself!"

Cold washed over him. He flashed in and out of existence, becoming visible and invisible over and over. His state, and that of the others, settled on visible; the magic of their silk veils had been counteracted.

Rither Pleagau—a middle-aged man with a thick, brown beard—studied his blades. He looked from Anthony Sizle, to Gelan Tryden Tris—the third in his lineage to be named as such—and to Emery Manden.

Sizle was the smallest. He had a young and smooth face, with soft, brown hair, a couple pacs long. His light-blue eyes darted back and forth, scanning all the dark corners.

Tryden was older than Sizle, but younger than Rither. He had a worn-out, yet handsome face, framed with long, black hair cascading to his shoulders. He had his striking, green eyes fixed on Rither, awaiting his command.

Emery was the largest of all and a fearsome-looking man. He appeared violent and came across as callous, but Rither knew his heart was kind. Emery was Rither's age, but was far from handsome; he might have been at one time, but his face was covered in scars from battles past. He had a thick, red-brown beard. Greasy, red-brown hair hung down to his shoulders in a scruffy way.

All four stood there, visible and with their swords drawn, waiting for whomever they were exposed by to make a move, reveal himself.

"Welcome to my home," the voice said. "Let me introduce myself. I am, as you may know, Angus Kritz. This fine fort—Fort Lockdown—is my home. Granted, it has not been that for long, but I think it is rude to barge in without knocking. Don't you?"

Rither Pleagau stepped forward, and pointed his sword to the shadows the voice had come from. "Angus Kritz, known conspirator against the mortal realm and the Gods, I place you under arrest for your heinous crimes. Come peacefully, and we will not kill you... yet."

Angus Kritz laughed; it was a laugh that sent cold up and down one's spine in an endless barrage. The air got denser with magic. "You think you can kill me!? Here!?"

Rither clenched his jaw, and tightened his grip of the hilt of his sword. "What does it matter if it is here or somewhere else? What's special about this place? Why are you here?"

"Oh, dear... my dear, dear blades. You know so little, yet

you think you know so much. You know nothing of the true nature of your 'gods'. You haven't felt the power of the True God, Drahc Uhr. Worry not, friends, you will soon know His power, and the power of this place; that is a promise."

"Kritz, surrender now, or we will attack. This is your final warning," Rither offered with a growl.

Emery took a brash step ahead, looked into the dark, and faced Rither. "Can't we just kill him? Cutter is thirsty."

"Who's Cutter?" Sizle asked.

Emery grunted. "My sword, of course. It longs to delve into flesh."

With a sigh, Tryden closed his eyes and shook his head. "What have I told you, Brother Sizle? When Emery speaks, don't ask. Just don't ask."

"What the fuck do you mean by that!?" Emery snarled.

Rither cleared his throat, instantly quieting them. "What is your choice, Kritz? Death or captivity?"

Kritz stepped to the edge of the shadows. His sinister face was just out of sight, but Rither thought he saw a grin. And then Kritz unleashed a blue orb of magic. It soared forward with a crackle. The air it passed became electric.

Rither had to throw himself to the ground to avoid it, the others following his example. They got up, and rushed for Angus Kritz. Before they could get to him, eight soldiers clad in black leather armor covering their entire bodies jumped out of the shadows above.

Kritz disappeared into the hallway leading farther into the fort as the others prepared to fight. The blades placed themselves in a line, and the acrobatic soldiers in another, ready to spill blood.

The hostile soldiers dashed forward. The blades waited for them to come. When in range, one foe engaged them each, while the other four jumped high into the air, landing on the opposite side; they had the blades surrounded.

Rither ducked down as a sword was swung at him, and in an effort to break free, he dashed for one of the two he was combating. Smashing into him, they fell down.

Pushing himself up, Rither swung his sword back, slicing

11

open the foe behind him. Blood and insides flooded out and splashed over him. He spun around, just in time to parry a blow from the soldier he had pushed.

Tryden and Sizle stood back to back, fighting three enemy soldiers. They spun around, constantly making sure to keep a sword between themselves and the foes. It was hard; the hostiles jumped into the dark, only to land where the guardian blades weren't facing.

Tryden advanced toward one, stabbing with his sword. He felt the blade sink into its target's side. As the soldier stumbled away, Tryden noticed another coming for him. Quickly, he slashed with his sword in that direction, but too late; the enemy's blade cut into his side, spilling his blood and sending searing pain through him.

The third hostile slashed at Sizle, who blocked. Before he could counter, a sword broke free from the foe's belly, blood spattering on Sizle. As the foe fell, Emery faced the three he had initially fought, all of whom were recovering.

He walked to the closest one. He had not gotten up on his feet, and never got the chance; Cutter slashed through him, splitting him in two separate halves and spilling his insides onto the floor. The other two had gotten up, but hadn't regained their bearings. Emery cut open one with ease.

The last one looked from one of his dead brothers in arms to the other, and then to Emery. He swung about his sword, nearing his foe. Emery looked at him. Then the swing came; the enemy swung his sword, but Emery knocked the blade out of his hand with a swipe of his. The sword landed with a clang a couple leaps away.

The foe backed away, stumbling to his back. Emery could not help feeling sorry for him, but only for a second. When that moment was up, all bets were off.

Tryden's sword went through the man he injured earlier. The man flexed, and then went limp. Dropping the corpse to the ground, he and Sizle set their gazes upon their last foe. Before they could advance toward him, he jumped into the shadows above.

"Come back here, you coward!" Emery called out. "Cutter

longs for you, too!"

Having sliced through his second and final foe, Rither set his gaze upon the passageway leading farther into the fort, rather than the darkness above. "Emery, we are not here for these soldiers."

"I know, boss," Emery grunted. "I'd still like to remove all of them from existence. They're dangerous. They could hurt people in the future."

"I know that, Emery, but our focus should be on Kritz. He is much worse than any one soldier could ever be."

"I agree with Master Pleagau," Tryden panted, pressing a hand against his bloodied side. "We should move on."

From the dark, the final enemy came with deadly intent. Emery placed Cutter in between the foe's swing and Sizle's head. He took hold of the foe, and pulled him close. With his teeth bared and their eyes connected, he pushed Cutter into the masked warrior, and then let the lifeless body fall to the ground.

Sizle took a step back. "Holy shit! That was close! Thanks, Brother Emery."

Before Emery had time to say anything, he was cut short by a scream. Tryden fell down, and blinked at the darkness above. He grunted, and pressed his hands against his side.

"Master," he panted, "go on without me. One of the bastards stabbed me."

Rither crouched down, and examined his wound. He met Tryden's eyes with a smile. "Gelan, do not be an idiot. It is a flesh wound."

"Boss, here," Emery said, holding out a bit of blue moss. "Dew moss."

"Thank you, Emery." Rither seized the moss. He applied it to the wound, making Tryden gasp, and wrapped bandages around. "The pain will be worse at first, Gelan, but the dew moss will soon take it away and heal the wound."

Tryden lay down, panting deeply. "I think I'm okay. Could you guys help me up?"

The others laughed, relieved their friend hadn't perished. All three took hold of him and helped him up.

"Tryden, I need you to know, I'd never leave you behind," Rither said. He looked each of his three blades in the eyes. "I'd never leave any of you behind. Being part of the Guardian Blades means you're brothers with all other members. We're family, and that bond is what assures our victory."

"Well said, boss," Emery agreed.

With a warm smile, Rither let his eyes fall upon each of his guardian blades, before facing the darkness leading farther into the fort. "Let's get that bastard Kritz."

With their bloodstained swords at the ready, and a look of caution ahead, the guardian blades moved into the shadowy passageway. Anything could be hiding in those shadows—anything.

2

Torches lit up on both sides. They burned with blue flames, but Rither was glad to have the light. Inscriptions lined the hallway—creatures, people, things, and words. Rither studied them as he moved ahead, with Emery, Tryden, and Sizle right behind him.

"These carvings must tell a tale, perhaps the story of this fort," Tryden said. "See, it starts with this dragon."

He pointed to a magnificent carving of a dragon, standing on its hind legs with its wings spread wide. Humans bowed down below it. "The Dragon War. This feels like the Wall of Stories at the Temple of the Precursors."

Sizle looked to him with a frown. "The Dragon War? Why would they carve something about that here?"

"If we continue to look at the inscriptions, perhaps we will find out."

Rither moved on slowly. The next carving showed humans building the fort. Dragons towering up above kept vigil over their slaves. But his eyes caught the symbol beneath.

It had four lines, one to the left and three to the right in a column leaning toward the symbol's center. The left one was longer than the others and curved out to the lower left. The two lower ones on the right were curved to the lower right, and the upper one was curved to the upper left.

"What's that symbol?" Emery wondered.

"It is the symbol for Oblivion," Tryden said. "Why is it beneath the fort?"

Rither tore his stare from the carving. "I don't know."

The engravings that followed were of dragons cowering as humans charged against them. Then humans held up their swords in celebration of victory.

"The end of the Dragon War?" Sizle asked. "When we beat the dragons and took back our freedom?"

"Indeed," Tryden said. "So the fort has a lot to do with the Dragon War. It must have been built during the reign of the dragons, and when they were defeated, the people who built this fort and were kept here celebrated their freedom."

After the inscriptions about the Dragon War, battles over the fort were depicted. In the end, it was ruined and forgotten. The next carvings took place thousands of years later. They showed aevira attacking humans, who rebuilt the fort for protection. Aevira attacked, but were repelled. Yet again, humans raised swords in celebration of victory.

"This must be a depiction of the aevira of Eeven conquering Dragora—the Dragonlands—and the subsequent White Resistance," Tryden said. "The fort was used then, too? I am astounded! I've seen nothing of this in the texts about our history. I've never even heard of this fort before."

"No one has been here for hundreds of years," Rither said. "Time vanquishes even the strongest of strongholds."

Emery snorted. "Can we move on? I ain't much for history lessons. I just wanna find that bastard, Kritz, and kill him. I wanna run my sword through his heart."

"I know you do, Brother Emery," Tryden said, "but history is important; there are plenty of things we can learn from it. Look to the past to learn about the future."

"Then bury yourself in a book when we ain't on a mission, bookworm. Your smartass, Gods-damned remarks ain't got no place here in the field."

"I am not a bookworm; I am well read. I promise there will

come a day when my knowledge will be of use to us. Brains will always conquer brawn, in the end. The soldiers can flex their muscles all they want, but the well-thought-out tactics of the generals are what win the war."

"Emery, Gelan, stop bickering. I don't want to have to tell you again," Rither said. "Let's read the wall, and then move on. Don't worry, Emery, we'll get him."

"I'm sorry," Sizle said, "but why is it you're so eager to get this guy?"

"He is a worshipper of Drahc Uhr. We can't let people who get in bed with demons be free, can we?" Emery said, thinking it would put an end to the topic.

"There must be more to it. No one I've ever known is this passionate, adamant even, about their job."

Emery walked to Sizle, his massive stature to Sizle's small one. "Who says you know me!?"

"EMERY!" Rither snapped. "He asked a simple question. I said you needn't worry; we'll get him."

Emery breathed heavily, calming himself, and put a hand on Sizle's shoulder. "Sorry, little man. I ain't used to having friends. Boss is the only one I have."

Sizle smiled, although merely vaguely as Emery's massive size still intimidated him. "I'd like to be friends."

Emery sighed. "I'll tell you why I want Kritz so badly, but not now, kid."

"Let's continue checking the wall," Tryden said.

They moved along the wall. Aevira led to the fort by armed humans were carved into it. Tryden muttered about prisoners of war as he let his fingers graze the wall. Inscriptions of humans leaving the fort followed, and then ones of the fort falling into disrepair.

"Strange," Tryden muttered.

"What is, Brother Tryden?" Rither wondered.

"Well... Aevira—prisoners of war—were taken here, to this fort, right?" When the others agreed, Tryden continued. "We see humans leave and the fort fall into disrepair. We never see aevira leave. They could've been omitted, but I'm not so sure. Perhaps they were left here when their captors departed. It seems strange, cruel."

"You ain't saying they deserved better!?" Emery shouted. "They butchered and enslaved our people! Were it up to me, we'd sail across the Great Ocean and butcher them back!"

"You should realize that because one kingdom goes to war with another, it does not mean all citizens of that kingdom agree with it. It is not always they have a choice. Besides, all I'm saying is that humans usually aren't so cruel as to leave prisoners to starve to death. Perhaps the prisoners were not left alive."

Rither gave both of them a sharp look. "You're both being naive; humans have done plenty of things more awful than letting prisoners starve to death. You should consider yourselves lucky to live in the Empire, where acts of unimaginable horror are not committed—at least not publicly. Neither humans nor aevira are without blood on their hands in this long feud between the species."

"What's this engraving anyway?" Sizle asked, interrupting Tryden, who had opened his mouth to say something.

He stared at the very last inscription. It was a silhouette of a person. If it was Aeviri or human was indistinguishable. The person looked unnatural, sinister.

"There are Aeviri letters. They look newer than the rest," Sizle continued, running his fingers along text underneath the figure. "My pronunciation may be off, but I think it says, 'Biaktae tah ansenta mas'plu'."

"It means, 'Beware the ancient ones'," Rither translated. "Why is it written in Aeviri?"

"As Brother Sizle said, it is newer," Tryden said. "Perhaps some aevira came in search of treasure or information about an ancestor, but instead found something else—something they wished they hadn't."

Rither's eyes moved to the sinister figure carved into the stone wall. Whatever it was, it made him shudder. He forced his attention off of it. "Let's move on. We've wasted enough time here."

3

The end of the long, blue-lit hallway came into view. They had hiked for a half hour, down stairways, around corners, and along seemingly endless corridors. Now, light met their eyes, brighter than they had gotten used to, but still as cold and soft.

Reaching it, they could do nothing but stop and gaze into the room beyond; it was so vast, the ceiling, floor, and walls were shrouded in blackness, too far off for the eye to catch. A crossroads of three walkways led from the platform in the room's center to the wall they had just come out of and two distant corners. The platform was supported by a thick pillar, reaching down. The room felt older than the first section of the fort. The atmosphere was heavier.

The blades moved along the walkway, toward the platform in the center. It took several minutes to move the length of it and reach the platform. Once there, they sat down to rest for a while.

"This place is big," Tryden exhaled. "Really, really big."

Emery still stood up, looking at the others gasping for air on the ground. "Oh, come on, don't be such weaklings."

"Weaklings!?" Sizle objected. "We've been walking for half an hour! Before that, we fought those crazy ninja guys. Before that, we traveled for hours to find this fort. We are also carrying all this equipment."

"Our equipment ain't heavy, little guy. You should be glad we wear armor made of leather and cloud iron; both of those materials are light, but cloud iron is strong. When I was in the Imperial Legion, I had metal armor. It weighed five times as much, and we marched for hours on end."

Rither got up on his feet and examined the area while the others continued to argue. In the middle of the platform, a spiral staircase led into darkness below. The two walkways leading from the platform ended with a tower each.

"Towers inside a fort?" Rither muttered. "That's new."

A strong, blue light shone from above; the blades had to shield their eyes with a hand to see. The light's source—a blue orb—descended slowly, resting a couple of leaps above the staircase. A beam of light reached from each of the two towers to the orb.

"What is that thing!?" Sizle cried out.

"I don't know," Rither said. "Now, calm down."

"Indeed, you should all calm down," a voice said from the orb. "Getting upset won't help any of us."

"Kritz, show yourself!" Rither roared.

The orb's strong light faded, revealing Angus Kritz inside. He was an old man, about sixty years of age. He wore dark robes, with a hood hung back. His white hair was short and thin. His face was wrinkly and sinister, as if a shadow darkened it. Rither met his eyes. They had no iris; only the black pupil dotted the white of the eyes.

The evil wizard looked at the blades with a condescending stare. "It is nice to finally meet face to face after having been chased by you for months."

"I guess nice is a question of opinion," Tryden said.

"What is that thing?" Sizle repeated, this time calmly.

"My dear, young friend, it is nothing lethal; it is merely a field of energy," Kritz said. "In it, I cannot be touched."

"Coward," Emery growled. "Come out and fight me man to man."

"Quiet, dog," Kritz growled back. He turned his attention to Rither. "I have a challenge for you. You've proved yourself to be quite the nuisance, and this way, I won't have to waste my time killing you myself."

Rither gave him a skewed look. "What challenge?"

Kritz gestured to the spiral staircase. "I am going down to the next level. The energy field around me will cover the hole when I descend. You'll have to break it."

"And how will we do that?" Tryden asked.

Kritz put a smirk on his face, and gave Tryden a lopsided look of contempt. "I am sorry, but I cannot do everything for you. Figure it out yourself, you insolent wretch."

With a growl, Emery took off toward Kritz. The protective

bubble glowed brighter and expanded. Emery ran right into it, instantly being repelled away forcefully. He hit the floor a few leaps away, and groaned.

Rither clenched his fists so the knuckles whitened. "I will beat the challenge, and you'll answer for your crimes!"

"It is not I who am the criminal," Kritz replied. "I summon Maenics, you kill them; that makes you the criminal, Master Blade. You blindly follow the wrong gods."

Still in the bubble, Kritz descended into the hole with the staircase. The bubble flattened out, remaining as a barrier blocking the hole; there was no way down.

Emery pushed himself to his feet. "Now what, boss?"

"I don't know," Rither admitted.

"The beams! Do you see those beams?" Tryden pointed to the energy beams between the towers and the barrier. "Two beams connect to the barrier, one from each tower."

Rither let his eyes wander along the beams to the towers. "You think we must destroy some kind of power source?"

"Yes, Master Pleagau. I believe so."

Rither set his gaze upon the first of the two towers. "Then let's get to it."

4

They had entered the first of the two towers, and were trying to find a way to get up to where its energy beam originated from, but it was hard to find anything in the dark. The area was damper than the rest of the fort. The gravity—the sense of magic—was heavier.

They held out their hands to make sure not to walk into a wall. Rither's heart raced rapidly; the sense of magic scared him senseless. It was more powerful than anything he had ever felt, more so than any one wizard could ever be. Angus Kritz could not be the source of the power, so what was?

"Master," Sizle said with a tremble, "something is here."

They stopped dead in their tracks. Sizle was a few paces ahead of the others.

"What is it, Brother Sizle?" Rither asked.

"I-I t-touched s-something." Sizle was now well behind the others. "Something scaly and warm. It felt alive."

Torches lit up all along the hallway with cold, blue flames. The sharp features of a beast appeared, a fearsomely great reptile. From the tip of its long snout to the tip of its much longer tail, the beast was several leaps long. A line of spikes reached along its entire body.

It had two hind legs, and the arms at its front ended in a four-fingered hand with a fifth finger continuing as far as the arm. A membrane was attached to the fingertip and reached along the length of the arm to the body to form a wing, folded up by the elongated finger. The snout had teeth ready to carve through flesh.

The men unsheathed their swords, and held them toward the beast. It remained motionless, like it was unafraid of the four blades' blades.

Emery glanced at Rither. "What's going on, boss?"

Rither took a few careful steps forward, and smacked the beast with his sword. It remained still. "It is not alive; it is a statue."

They let the swords rest with the tips on the ground, and studied the statue.

Emery shoved Sizle gently. "Good job, Brother Sizle."

Rither put his hand on the beast. "Don't blame Sizle; it is hot to the touch, just like he said. It looks remarkably alive, too; it fooled us all."

Emery snorted. "I guess you are right, boss. What kind of beast is this anyways?"

Tryden put a sly smile on his face. "Isn't it obvious? It's a dragon—a statue of one, anyway."

"Guess I didn't recognize it 'cause it ain't a crappy drawing on some flat wall in a ruined fort at a random location in the Cyran wilds that ain't been visited in a couple hundred years and no one will care to visit again in the next hundred years," Emery said, all in one breath.

After a few moments, he added, "Alright, I take back that last part, about the ruined fort and so forth; after all, it is in a ruined fort."

Sizle moved to the dragon statue, and put his hand on it. "A dragon!? Wow! I have never seen one like this before. It is three-dimensional and so lifelike."

"Most people haven't," Tryden said. "I've seen a statue like this before, though, a long time ago."

Emery rolled his eyes. "Wow, you've seen a rock shaped as a big lizard. Good for you."

Rither smirked at the comment. It was just so like Emery; he wasn't a thinker, but a doer. Tryden was the opposite; he was a thinker. It was why Rither liked having both of them on his team. Though they did not realize it, they worked well together.

Tryden glared at Emery. "Brother Emery, you seem not to realize that knowledge and culture are important. I'd go as far as say that, in battle, knowledge is more important than skill with a sword. If you know your enemy, you can defeat him, regardless of how technically skilled he is. Brains over brawn, is what I say."

Emery stared right back. "Okay, your highness, whatever you say."

Tryden clenched his jaw, and his countenance turned into ice. "Whatever I was in my past, I am no longer. I cannot return to the Trydan Kingdom. You know that."

"Then why do you act like it? Only nobles think an enemy can be defeated with books. I don't deny the importance of brains, but they can't be obtained by reading; they must be learned through live combat."

Rither gave the two a sidelong glance. "Simmer down, you two. You are more alike than you know."

Emery faced him. "Excuse me, boss!?"

"You burn so hot with passion for what you believe in. It's quite amusing listening to you argue. If I didn't know you so well, if I didn't know deep down you're actually good friends, I'd think you hate each other. I would've stopped your bickering sooner, and I would've disciplined you."

"Maybe you don't know us as good as you think, boss."

"Emery, please. How long have I known you? For almost

ten years now. And how long have we known Tryden? Three years now, Emery. We've known him for three years. I know both of you well."

"Sorry, guys, but I can't help feeling a little left out here," Sizle said.

Rither cocked his head to the side, and put a sympathetic smile on his face. "You're new, Brother Sizle. Give it time."

Sizle did not answer. Instead, he looked into the darkness ahead. "Did you guys hear that?"

"Don't try to scare us again, brother runt," Emery said. "It ain't gonna work a second time."

"No, I'm serious. Quiet down. Listen."

Rither and the others kept quiet. Sizle was right. An odd sound—soft and high-pitched, like faint screeching—came from up ahead.

"What do you think that is?" Sizle asked.

"I don't know," Rither replied, "but we'll soon find out."

He moved through the light around the statue toward the darkness beyond. Reaching the edge of light, torches lit up, casting light ahead of him. Moving farther, more torches lit up, always leaving the area just in front of him dark.

The three other blades followed him, now through a field of light. They all had tight grips of their swords. They didn't know what lurked ahead, where the torches were unlit.

They slowly took one step onward at a time. Rither felt his heart pounding once again. He was sure the others felt the same, regardless of if they would admit it. He would never admit it himself; he was a leader; he needed to seem invincible to his followers.

The screeching had gone on for a few minutes, but had now turned into dead silence. Only Sizle's soft footsteps and breathing were heard. Every soft thud ripped into Rither; he disliked that they were not quiet, especially when something lurked about and they were without their silk veils.

At the hallway's end, stairs led them to the second floor. Judging by its height and the height of the ceiling, the tower had three levels. They had one more to go through to reach the source of the energy beam.

Infrequent torches lit up patches of the darkness as they strode ahead. Rither didn't like it; he liked the light, but had never been a fan of magic. It terrified him. It was one of the reasons he joined the Guardian Blades—to bring justice to evil gifted ones. The darkness up ahead frightened him even more; something was there, quiet but definitely there.

Far into the shroud ahead, Rither spotted a torch casting light on the stairs up.

Soft, rapid footsteps echoed through the hallway from behind. More footsteps in front of them, just outside their line of sight. Screeches and hisses sounded from the dark. The footsteps were all around, always just out of sight. Whatever was hiding in the shadows was toying with them, poisoning them with fear. It would not work; blades felt fear, but never let it affect them.

"Come on, you freaks," Emery growled. "Attack us!"

As if antagonized, a reptilian beast lunged at him. It stood on two thick and muscular legs, had a couple of thin arms, and had an angled posture. From the tip of its short snout to the tip of its long tail, it was a leap long. The scales covering its body were light brown. It had sharp claws and teeth. A majestic shield of bone and scales encircled and reached up above its head.

Emery swung his sword in a sideways arc, beheading the reptile. Black blood and the severed head followed the sword as it finished its arc. He caught the lifeless—and headless—body still coming at him, and threw it to the side. "Clav, an infernal reptile from Oblivion."

"A Beast Maenic," Sizle stammered.

"That is not a clav," Tryden corrected them. "It's a clavi, a cousin to the clav indigenous to Siva."

Sizle shuddered visibly. "There is a cousin to the clav here in the mortal plane of existence?"

"How do you know?" Emery asked.

"Clav are bigger and fiercer; it's easily three times the size of a clavi," Tryden stated. "And yes, Brother Sizle, there is a cousin to the clav—called clavi—that lives here in Siva."

"No time to discuss the manner of creature we are facing,"

Rither intervened. "Let's move on to the staircase."

Another two clavi came at them. One crashed into Tryden and knocked him to the ground. He put out his left arm to shield himself from the bite, and felt its teeth sink into his flesh. The other jumped onto Rither, who remained upright as it held on to him with its surprisingly strong arms.

Sizle drove his sword into the one atop Tryden. It let go its bite, and let out a high-pitched squeal, before falling dead. Rither shoved away the one hanging on to him, and stepped on its neck before plunging his sword into its eye.

The four blades took off for the stairs as fast as possible. Several clavi chased them down. One or two of the reptiles, they could handle, but there were too many of them; dozens came from the shroud of shadows. Before they could reach the stairs, the quick and nimble clavi had surrounded them and cut them off in all directions.

"Let's fight them," Emery said.

Sizle let out a nervous laugh, as he spun about trying to keep track of the clavi. "Lucky us we only have to fight clavi, not clav. Am I right?"

The clavi stood around them, screeching softly. Between the men and the staircase, clavi stepped aside. Before they could dash through, a beast—similar to the clavi, but bigger and with blood-red scales—stepped through.

Tryden could not help but take a step away. "Now, that"— he swallowed—"is a clav. That is a Maenic."

Emery glared at Sizle. "You had to say something, didn't you? 'Lucky us', wah, wah, wah. Good job. You jinxed us."

As the clavi widened the circle, the clav remained still. Its orange eyes—glowing like fire—were fixed on Rither. It was a fearsome beast, four leaps from the tip of its snout to the tip of its tail. Even with its angled posture, it stood much taller than the men. Veins were visible on its shield, and a horn of bone shot out of its forehead.

The clav dashed forward headfirst, with its horn pointing at Rither. He dodged it, but was knocked down by the bony shield. Sizle came at the creature from behind, but it spun around and threw its entire weight at him, knocking him to the ground, too.

The clav launched itself toward Tryden and Emery. Emery stood his ground; he never backed out of a fight, no matter what. Tryden grabbed hold of him, and dragged him down, avoiding the death-dealing strike from the clav's horn by the width of a hair. Emery shoved Tryden off of himself.

Clavi sprinted from the circle to Rither and Sizle, cutting them off from Tryden and Emery. Clavi after clavi dashed to them, and were cut down by one of the two blades. The floor was filling up with thick, black blood and body parts.

Tryden and Emery were left alone by the clavi. They were fighting the clav, the larger and fiercer beast. They circled it, as the clavi that had now formed a new circle around them looked on.

"Okay, Brother Emery," Tryden said, "if we work together, we can take this thing down."

Emery snorted. "Talk for yourself, brother bookworm. I'm taking it down. I don't need anyone's help, let alone yours."

"Do not be an idiot. It is too strong. Its hide is too strong. You won't hurt it, unless you hit it in the right places."

With a roar, Emery charged at the clav. Having looked at Tryden, the reptile spun around and threw itself at Emery, horn first. He avoided the horn, but was knocked down by the shield.

He got up, and attacked it again, landing a successful hit. Its hide was—like Tryden had predicted—too strong for the sword. The clav knocked Emery to the ground once more.

"Damn it, listen to me!" Tryden bellowed as he dodged the clav's tail. "We've got to work together!"

Emery growled as he got up on his feet. "I doubt there is anything you can do. Books can't teach you everything."

"We should learn from those who know better. It is one of our duties as knights of the Guardian Blades."

"I also doubt that a bookworm who wrote a book has any substantial experience; it's all theory."

Tryden clenched his jaw; he was tiring of Emery's dense-ness. "Master Pleagau's authored a book. Do you think he is an inexperienced bookworm, too?"

"Of course not. He's the one person I respect in the whole world. I—" Emery paused. "Maybe you're right. What do you know about clav?"

"A book I've read said, while the clav has skin superior to any non-magical blade, it's got a soft spot at the base of its neck, behind its shield."

"Well, that's awesome," Emery said while rolling his eyes. "All we have to do is climb up on the giant and deadly beast. That sounds so easy."

Tryden smiled, dodging the clav's tail again. "Exactly."

The clav dashed to Emery. He scarcely avoided the horn, but was once again knocked down by its shield. "This thing is pissing me off!"

"I'll distract it. You climb up on its back and stab it in its soft spot," Tryden said, turning to the beast. "Hey, you big, ugly thing!" He neared the reptile, and swung his sword, but backed off as it threw its snout full of sharp teeth at him.

Emery snuck around its back. With a secure grip around the hilt of his sword, he leapt onto the reptile. The clav, previously preoccupied with Tryden, started thrashing about to get him off of it in a frenzy of rage and panic.

"Kill it!" Tryden shouted.

Emery tried to hold on, but it proved even harder than he had imagined. Even so, he held on and crawled closer to the back of its head. He raised his sword to finish it. One of the clavi leapt over the clav and rammed Emery. He dropped the sword, but held on to the clav.

"My sword!" he cried out. "I dropped my damn sword!"

Several clavi closed in on Tryden. He had nowhere to run. He looked at them, and then at Emery, who was hanging on to the clav for his life. "Brother Emery, here!" He threw his sword to Emery, and prepared for what was to come as the clavi closed in.

Emery caught the sword, and thrust it into the clav's soft spot, at the base of the back of its neck. Black blood spouted out, and when he pulled out the sword, even more burst out. With a squeal, the clav swirled around, knocking about clavi, before crashing to the ground.

All clavi started running around sporadically, crashing into each other and the men. Eventually, the last of them vanished into the shadows, leaving behind nothing but an echo of their footsteps, and then silence.

Emery jumped off of the Beast Maenic's carcass. "Tryden, you okay!?"

Tryden stood still at first, seemingly paralyzed, or as if he hadn't heard. He met Emery's eyes, and just nodded.

"Why did you do that!? You could've died!"

Tryden swallowed his shock and fear. "I knew I could not kill that many clavi by myself, and I thought they might get scared if you killed the clav."

"You were right," Emery said, scanning the shadows. "The clavi are all gone."

Tryden managed to get a smirk on his face. "Yeah. Maybe I should write a book about it."

5

The room at the tower's top was vast. Its walls reached high, but carried no roof, merely darkness. In the middle, a pillar reached high above the walls, and a staircase spiraled up its side. A crystal atop the pillar seemed to be the power source for the barrier, emitting a blue beam over the walls. Prison cells lined the back wall.

Rither moved toward the pillar. "Let's destroy the crystal."

"Stop right there, you filthy mortals." The voice was high-pitched, throaty, and hissing, with an undertone that could only be called darkness. "You should not play with powers you do not quite understand."

Rither spun around and around. "Who's there!?"

Black smoke appeared from nowhere, placing itself in between the blades and the pillar. The smoke soon took shape and became solid.

The seemingly male being was humanoid and as tall as a man, but looked bigger. Its skin was black and smooth. Its features were sharp and chiseled. It had five clawed fingers and four clawed toes, three at the front of the foot and one at the back. It wore jagged, red armor, made of a metal unknown to Rither. It was a Maenic, a true Maenic.

It grinned. "I am J'da, one of the Lesser Maenics. Don't let my species fool you; there's nothing lesser about me. I'm far superior to all of you mortal life forms."

"I beg to differ," Tryden retorted.

J'da laughed; it was the kind that chilled one's blood and sent shivers down one's spine. "You may... beg, that is."

Tryden waited for the Maenic to stop its manic laughing. "Maenics are inferior, or lesser as you said. We mortals have the Gods on our side."

"Maybe you shouldn't antagonize it," Sizle whispered behind Tryden.

"Step aside, you unholy beast, or we will slay you," Rither demanded.

J'da stood its ground, wrapping its arms around itself to feign fright. "Oh no, the mortals will slay the immortal! I am so scared!"

"You should be! We will send you back to Oblivion, where you can continue your wretched, immortal life!"

"Even if you do, I will come back. Even if you defeat me a thousand times, I will come back. My master will win in the end; it is inevitable."

Sizle tried to take a confident step forward, but ended up lifting his foot and placing it in the same spot. "You won't! The barrier between Oblivion and Siva protects us."

"It won't if Oblivion is brought here," J'da stated. "It won't do any good if it is broken down either."

"What do you mean?" Tryden asked. "Oblivion cannot be brought to Siva because of the barrier, which can't be broken down. Not even your wicked master can do that."

"That is incorrect," J'da said with a demonic smile full of sharp teeth. "Lord Uhr cannot bring down the barrier from Oblivion; from Siva is another thing altogether."

"Be that as it may, Drahc Uhr can't come to Siva with the barrier up, so He can't bring it down."

"Only His magic needs to be brought here."

"But that's not possible either!"

J'da chuckled and gave Tryden a lopsided look, and then faced Rither. "I can't let you destroy the crystal. Although it is too late to stop us, it is stupid to take chances. Besides, I would not want to leave without the pleasure of ripping your spines right out of your puny bodies."

J'da held its arms in ninety-degree angles from its body. Smoke appeared by its hands, and took shape. The smoke by its left hand became a black and red shield, with sharp corners and spikes. The smoke by its right hand became a serrated sword, its hilt black and its blade black and red.

The Maenic moved to the men. Sizle stood frozen in fear. Tryden also stood still, but fingered his sword's hilt, waiting to engage in battle. Rither and Emery had already faced off against Maenics before, and were steadier.

J'da swung its sword in an arc toward Rither. He instantly raised his own to parry the Maenic's attack. Emery then came at it, swinging his sword. The Maenic raised its shield to parry, before pushing him away with it.

Tryden carefully tried to stab it, but it blocked the attack with its shield. It swung its sword sideways at Rither, who ducked to avoid. With a screech, the Maenic sent out a force wave, knocking all blades down on the ground.

J'da looked at the knocked-over men with a grim look on its twisted face. "This really isn't fair, is it? Let us battle, one at a time." It swiped its arm sideways, and everyone except Tryden froze in their current movements.

Tryden crawled to his feet, and looked to his brothers in arms, before facing the Maenic. "What did you do!?"

"Do not worry, little mortal, they're paralyzed, most likely temporarily."

Tryden backed away as the Maenic slashed at him. Fear spread through him with every beat of his heart, every slash of the Maenic's sword. J'da knocked Tryden's sword out of his hand. His left arm was weak after the bite, so he could only use his right arm, not his sword arm.

"Tryden," Rither squeezed out, "you can do it. Just... believe in yourself."

"Ah, how cute. Your friend believes in you," J'da taunted. "It is quite admirable actually; it takes a lot of willpower to break free from my magic."

The Maenic was right, even if it meant it differently; it was admirable. Tryden couldn't let down his blade brothers. He wouldn't let them down.

The demon's sword came for him. He rolled away, dodging the lethal strike. Getting back on his feet, he looked for his sword. It wasn't too far away; he could make it there before J'da would have time to catch up and end it.

He ran toward the sword as quickly as he could. He could sense the Maenic right behind him. He rolled to the sword, grabbed it, and raised it to parry a deadly attack.

With a growl, Tryden tackled the demon. He would not let Sizle down. He hit the Maenic hard, sending its sword flying. He would not let Emery down. He hit the Maenic hard, sending its shield flying. The demon sank to its knees, and hissed through gritted teeth. Tryden met its black eyes. He would not let down his master.

With a sideways swipe, Tryden severed the Maenic's head from its body. As the head rolled to a dark corner, the body fell over with a clank, washing black blood all over.

Tryden had killed the Maenic. He had sent its unholy soul back whence it had come—the fiery depths of Oblivion. The magic holding his comrades was lifted. Sizle insisted on fist bumping him, while Emery just nodded.

Rither put an arm around his shoulder, as they headed to the pillar with the crystal. "I am proud of you, Tryden. You really came through, in this battle and against the clav. You and Emery put aside your differences, even though he was resistant at first."

"Thanks, Master Pleagau." Tryden put a smile on his face, but it quickly turned into a clenched frown. "Master, could I have more dew moss? A clavi bit me, the little bugger."

"Emery, give Tryden more dew moss, and I will go destroy the crystal."

Rither headed up the stairway spiraling around the pillar. Reaching the top, he stepped onto a platform just a couple of leaps across, above which the man-sized crystal hovered. He stared at the ominous, blue glow of the crystal for a few moments. Then, with a secure grip of his sword, he slashed at it with all his might.

The gemstone exploded into a million pieces, flying in all directions. The cloud iron of his armor absorbed the splinters, but each little fragment knocked the air out of him. An orb floating in the air was all that remained in the crystal's absence. It was peaceful, in harmony.

The light started moving about in a whirlwind. Faster and faster, it spun around, the light intensifying by the second. Rither sprinted down the staircase. The twister of light spun inward, becoming a singularity.

He had just gotten down the stairs as the singularity expanded rapidly. The pillar was shattered, and the explosion knocked all blades off their feet. Heavy rocks crashed down, breaking against the solid ground.

Destruction rang in Rither's ears, as he tumbled about in an attempt to stand. He heard a voice. He focused on it; he tried to use it as a beacon to steady himself.

"Hey, you guys! Over here!"

Someone was indeed calling out. Rither looked about, before resting his eyes on the prison cells. He moved to them, with the other blades right behind him.

Two young men were locked in a cell. One was filthy and wild, with gray, scruffy hair. His torn clothes were as dirty as the rest of him. The other was well-groomed, with a kind face and long, blond hair. He wore dark robes.

"Who are you?" Rither asked them.

"Oh, I apologize. Where are my manners, good sirs?" The well-groomed man bowed. "I am Rynus Kalera, a wizard in training. This... lowly wretch is Adam Kalera, my good-for-nothing cousin."

Rither looked from one to the other. Gesturing to himself and the men under his command, he said, "I am Sir Rither Pleagau, blade master of the Guardian Blades of Siva. That young fellow is Sir Anthony Sizle, the suave man over there is Sir Gelan Tryden, and that big guy is Sir Emery Manden, all blade brothers."

"So you people are guardian blades, huh?" Rynus stated, more than asked. "I suppose you're here to stop my mast—" A short pause. "Angus Kritz."

Emery took a brash step forward, and pointed his sword at the man, Rynus Kalera. "Kritz is your master!?"

"Well, yes. No. I mean, he was, but not anymore. Please, let us out. There is a lever outside the cell. I'd pull it myself, with magic, but it is shielded. We can help you stop Kritz."

Rither crossed his arms below his chest. "How?"

"I know this place; I've spent a lot of time here. My magic can be of use to you and if I were against you, I'd simply kill you through these bars."

Rither stared Rynus right in the eyes. "Okay, but I'll keep my eye on you. If I doubt your loyalty, even for a second, I'll make sure you're a head shorter."

Rynus held out a hand between the metal bars of the cell. "I accept your terms."

6

The inside of the second tower was just as dark and its atmosphere just as heavy with magic as the first tower. At the end of the long corridor, a lone torch revealed the staircase leading up. As the blades and Kalera cousins moved along the hallway, torches lit up with blue flames. Thick, red vines had grown on the stone walls, right through the ceiling.

They were of no consequence. The men just had to make their way to the third floor and destroy the second crystal so they could follow Angus Kritz and kill him. Rither clenched his fists at the memory of what Kritz had done.

"Kalera, may I ask you something?" Sizle said.

"No need to be formal. Use our names," Rynus answered. "And yes, you may."

"Oh, thanks. I wanted to ask why the two of you were in a cell. So that's what I'm doing. Why were you in a cell?"

Rynus cleared his throat. "I was, as I said, Kritz's disciple.

I... was going through a rough time. I wanted to rebel, to be somebody. When I learned what Kritz is doing here, I didn't want to be a part of it. He locked me up, in case I'd get any ideas, like telling someone of what he's doing."

"And... Adam is it? Why was he locked up?"

"Stupid as he is, he decided to rob my former master after I wrote to him about the amazing artifacts we've found here. Ancient swords and armor. Even gemstones and artifacts of magic."

"Yep. I was lock up-ed with cousin Rynus. We was all lock up-ed together. All two of us," Adam said, smiling a crooked smile. "Now that I'm free, I'll get me that treasure."

Sizle looked away to hide his quiet laughter. "I see."

"What is it your master is doing here?" Rither asked. "I'm guessing he's not here for the valuables."

"You wouldn't believe me if I told you," Rynus said.

"Try me," Rither retorted.

"Try us," Tryden corrected.

"He's bringing Oblivion here," Rynus said.

Tryden raised his eyebrows. "He is bringing Oblivion into Siva? That's not possible."

"Yes, it is," Rynus snorted. "Look, I cannot explain all of it, and to fully do so would take hours. Truth be told, I don't know all that much about it. But unless we stop him, we're all dead. I mean all of us, everyone that walks Atae."

"Me too?" Adam asked him.

Rynus shut his eyes, and rubbed them with a hand. "Yes. You too, Adam."

"Uhm, Rynus, what's wrong with him?" Emery whispered. "Is he a bit... soft in the head?"

Rynus looked at his cousin. "He is not retarded if that is what you are saying; he is illiterate. My parents died when I was young. My aunt and uncle, Adam's parents, took me in. After noticing my... talents, they forgot about Adam. Since they couldn't afford education for us both, I was selected to go to school while he got to work at the family farm."

"I see," Emery said, looking at Tryden, who met his eyes. "I can consider myself lucky to have been educated."

"Finally, you see things as I do! Education is important!" Tryden exclaimed, with a wide and smug grin. "But there is one more question mark. Education is free in Cyra—in the Empire—so you can't be from here. Where are you from?"

"The Kayan Kingdom," Rynus replied, Adam nodding beside him.

Rither frowned. "The Kingdom of the Kayan Isles? I have heard disturbing rumors about your king."

"Like what?" Sizle asked.

"He's executed people for expressing their opinion. I've also heard of racial and religious discrimination, among other things," Rither said. He turned to Rynus. "Is this true?"

"I'm afraid so," Rynus said, looking at the ground. "Since Lord Culous Alamain was murdered and the rightful heir to the Kayan throne was chased off forty-four years ago, things have been bad. There's a morbid sense of irony, though."

"How so?"

"Lord Culous's murderer was his youngest son Adrian. He was jealous of his brother, and wanted the throne for himself. Then his son Fendon murdered him for the throne. Two years ago, Fendon was killed by his son Raul."

Rither shook his head at all the bloodshed. "I'm sorry. I've heard the Kayan Isles were a paradise during Lord Culous's reign. I have also heard his other son, the lost crown prince, shared his qualities of kindness and compassion. The kingdom might have been better off with him as king."

Rynus smiled a sad smile. "We will never know. There are hopes the true heir to the throne will one day return and in a brief moment of justice behead this latest of false kings."

"Wouldn't the crown prince be around seventy or eighty?" Tryden asked. "If he's even alive, that is."

"It is said that before Adrian's betrayal, the crown prince had a child with an aevir. It is also said that he evaded the soldiers loyal to Adrian and has lived in peace somewhere, with this child," Rynus said, passion and hope burning hot in his voice. "It is said that his child, or perhaps grandchild, will one day return, and all will be well in the kingdom."

"I can only say that I hope it will be so," Rither said.

The six men fell silent as they continued through the corridor. They reached the staircase with no trouble, and headed to the second floor. It was dark as the night, and as they moved along it, no torches lit up.

"Here," Rynus said. He held up an arm, and his hand was set aflame, seemingly without hurting him. Its shallow light was not what Rither had hoped for, but better than nothing. "Stay close to me."

"Amazing!" Sizle commented.

They crept close to the wizard—Rynus—desperate to be in his circle of light, small as it may be. They then moved forward, through the pitch-dark corridor.

Rither noticed the floor was uneven, making it difficult to walk straight. Looking down, he saw the same vines as before. He also sensed something in the dark—something else entirely. It sent shivers down his spine.

"Uhm, guys," Rynus began, "I have lost track of where we came from and where we should go."

They stood in the dark. Rynus was right. Rither could not tell from where they had come. He had been so preoccupied watching his feet as he stumbled across the jungle of vines, he hadn't noticed where they were going.

He pointed in a direction. "We came from somewhere over there, I think. If we find a wall, we can just walk along it to where we're supposed to go. If we're wrong, we can just turn around."

They stumbled to—what they hoped was—the side of the room. When a wall met his eyes, Rither let out a sigh of relief. However, it was covered in vines so not a single particle of rock peeked through, which worried him.

"Be careful with the fire, Rynus," he said. "If you light up the vines, whatever they are, you may burn down more than the plants."

They headed in the direction Rither thought was the right one. He still had the sense something was in the darkness, but hoped they would find the way up before meeting whatever it was.

Something smooth brushed against his leg. He turned to

look for whatever had done it. He saw nothing but the wall of blackness around them.

"What is it, boss?" Emery asked. "Something wrong?"

"Something grazed against my leg," Rither answered.

"What?"

"Something."

"Master," Sizle said with a quiver, "could you wait up?"

"What is it, Brother Sizle?" Rither asked.

"It's my leg. It's... It's stuck," Sizle said, still with a quiver. "My damn leg is stuck! It won't come loose!"

Rynus bent down, holding his fire near Sizle. A vine had spun itself tightly around his leg. Rynus moved his arm to the others' legs. Vines were spun around all their legs; they were all stuck.

Sizle clawed at the vine holding on him. "What the hell are these things!? I want loose!"

"Calm down, Brother Sizle," Tryden said. "If we stay calm and think this through, we can—"

"Tryden!?" Sizle shouted. No answer came. "Gelan!?"

Rynus moved his arm, showering its light over Tryden. A thick vine had wrapped itself around his neck, like a snake. He was trying to get it off, but couldn't; it was too strong.

Rither went to help, but a vine wrapped itself to his arm, dragging him away. More vines came from the ceiling, wall, and floor, wrapping themselves around the men's necks and strangling them.

They desperately tried to fend off the vines, but with little success. Rither still had his sword arm free. He hacked and slashed at the vines. He managed to cut off the vine holding Tryden's neck, giving him a moment to breathe before a new one took its place.

A moan came from the dark, and the sound of something heavy being dragged across the ground followed. A human came into the light of Rynus's flame. Its half-rotten skin was covered in sores, and the jaw had fallen off. Its arms hung, almost lifeless, and its dead eyes were glazed white.

"It is a soulless one," Rynus managed to squeeze out, "an unholy, undead abomination."

"We need to get these vines off, now!" Rither struggled to say, as he continued to hack and slash at the vines.

More soulless ones entered the light. Their hungry, dead eyes stared at the men. One charged forth, half running and barely holding together. A swipe of Rither's sword cut off its arm. It staggered back as blood spouted out, but recovered its footing and headed for them again.

"Cut off its head!" Tryden squeezed out.

Rither swung his sword yet again, decapitating the rotten human. Its head flew away. Blood spouted out of its gaping neck as the body collapsed to the floor with a squish. Many more soulless ones stumbled over the body, on their way to the men.

Seeing the undead horde, Rither felt his heart sink. "It is no use! There are too many of them, and as soon as I cut off the vines, new ones take their places!"

"There's one thing I can do," Rynus squeezed out, "but it's somewhat crazy!"

Emery tore a vine from his neck, only to have another one take its place. "Do it!"

"But—"

"Do it!"

Rynus moved his fiery arm to the vines on the wall. They were set aflame. The fire spread along the vines, and lit up new ones. The ones holding them let go. Rither thought he could hear them screech, but it was impossible to tell in the ruckus.

They had to move quickly; the fire was spreading, and it could kill them just as easily as the vines and soulless ones could. They moved along an unlit corridor between the fires. The undead monsters ran through the fires, having been set aflame. They soon fell over, crisp and smoking.

A soulless one came at them. Emery knocked it back with the broad side of his sword, and then slashed it in two. The upper torso fell off, and the lower part fell to the floor, bowels spilling out all over.

They continued through the unlit path as fast as possible. The fire could stop their progress at any time. The room was now as bright as day, and they could see the stairs leading up. Just a few more paces remained to the stairway, but a blaze of fire blocked the pathway.

"We'll have to go through the fire!" Rither barked. "Go!"

Sizle, Tryden, and Emery jumped through the fire, one at a time. Rither urged Adam and Rynus to jump through.

Adam stood by the fire, staring into its blazing dance. The flames were reflected in his eyes. "Cousin, I doesn't thinks I can do it. I wants to go home."

"Of course you can, Adam," Rynus answered. "Just head through, quickly."

"This is way over me head, cousin. I ain't builded for this. Please, cousin, I wants to go back."

"No! We can only go forward. Please, just head through, Adam. I'll be right behind you. You won't be hurt."

Adam stared into the flames. Again, they were reflected in his cornea. He breathed in deeply, getting ready.

Seemingly from nowhere, an undead came. Rither quickly spun around and decapitated it. A second one pushed him to the ground, throwing itself onto him. He desperately tried fending it off. Saliva filled its rotten mouth. Its yellow teeth longed to bite into his flesh.

Adam dragged the soulless one off Rither. It spun around, and launched itself onto him instead. They fell down with a thud. It sank its sickening teeth into his shoulder. Its face was stained with blood. Its mouth was filled with a chunk of flesh. Adam screamed into the hazy air.

Rither ran his sword through the soulless one's head, and dragged away its corpse. Rynus fell to his knees beside his cousin. Crying and screaming, Adam grabbed hold of him, and they dragged him to his feet together. With their arms around each other, they moved through the fire.

Rither took a good look back. Soulless ones were burning in the fire, and numerous more had already been burned to a crisp and were oozing smoke. When he had had enough of the death, he followed the others, through the flames.

7

The upmost floor was akin, if not identical, to the same floor in the first tower; the only difference was that the cells here were empty. Just like in the first tower, a pillar reached up above the high walls, and a crystal emitted an energy beam over them.

Rither moved toward the pillar, followed by Anthony Sizle, Gelan Tryden Tris, Emery Manden, and Rynus Kalera, who had his arm around Adam Kalera. Bandages held dew moss in place over Adam's shoulder wound.

Well before reaching the pillar, a voice interrupted them, like in the first tower. It was also throaty and hissing, with an undertone of darkness, but it was not as high-pitched as the first one. "Mortals, welcome!"

Black smoke appeared, and soon took shape into another Maenic, also seemingly male. It looked even viler, more misshapen, than the prior one. It wore the same kind of armor, but already had a sword and shield ready.

The Maenic bowed, but kept its vigilant eyes on the men. "I am Krii, one of the Lesser Maenics."

"We know. We've already met one of you," Rither growled.

"Ah. Then you killed him? Good job!" The Maenic bowed again. "Although, it all depends on how you define 'kill'. You did destroy his physical shell here in Siva, but we Maenics don't really die in the same way as you mortals."

"We don't have time for this. Let us pass!"

Krii smiled crookedly with its ugly, sharp teeth. "Well that would be no fun at all, now would it? Don't you know anything about us Maenics? We looove to spill blood, yes we do. That we do. We love to do that. Don't you love it?"

Rither bared his teeth. "I bet you do. We don't like to spill blood, but sending Maenics back to their hellhole of a home is our specialty."

Krii jumped up and down, excited about the topic—death. "That's the spirit! Also, you do know I cannot let you break the crystal? Your chance of stopping us is slim, but it would be stupid to give you a sporting chance, now wouldn't it?"

Tryden smiled. "Doesn't it feel awful to have a human—a mortal—master?"

"If you're referring to the Angus Kritz character, then you are miserably mistaken, little mortal. I am not here to obey him; I am here to make sure he does his job. The only lord I have is Drahc Uhr. He is the True God, the god you should worship, filthy mortal."

"Let us pass, now!" Rither demanded.

"Let us fight, now!" Krii demanded right back.

Krii advanced on them. Rynus backed off, bringing Adam with him. Rither understood; he would have prioritized protecting a helpless relative, as well. It did not matter, though; four blades were more than a match for a Maenic.

Krii grinned. "Oh, by the way, look behind you."

Rither looked back, and saw soulless ones coming up the stairs. He could see the hunger in their dead eyes. "Damn it! Brothers Tryden and Sizle, hold off the soulless ones. Rynus can help you. Emery and I will take care of the freak."

"I have a name, you know," Krii taunted them. "I might be a Maenic, immortal and all, but I do have feelings."

Sizle and Tryden rushed back. They hacked and slashed, pushing the abominations to the staircase. They wanted to use it as a choke point, where only one or two soulless ones could come at a time. They had the slight aid of Rynus, who burned the soulless ones near him and his cousin.

Rither readied his sword. His heart pounded in his chest. He could only imagine what Emery felt. In fact, he couldn't. Emery was always calm in battle. His rough voice was rarely anything but calm. He was confident in every situation, and never scared. Rither hoped he was scared; he had learned through experience that fear could be a useful ally, as long as one didn't let it take control.

Krii bashed Rither with its shield, and swung its sword at Emery. He blocked its attack with his sword, and punched the Maenic hard. Krii stumbled back, spit out some blood, and advanced once more.

Before it could go on the offensive, Rither swept his sword vertically. Emery also attacked, with a sideways swipe. Krii blocked Rither's attack by raising its shield and Emery's by placing its sword with the blade down in between itself and Emery's sword. It swung its shield into Emery's chest, and knocked him to the ground.

Rither slashed at the Maenic, but it dodged and swung its own sword at him. Rither raised his sword to block the attack, feeling the power of the vicious demon. It was incredibly strong.

Emery rose to his feet behind the Maenic, and charged at it with his sword first. Krii dodged, swinging its shield into his face. Emery had built up quite the momentum, and flew forward, slamming down on the ground. He lay on his back, grunting in pain, with blood gushing out of his nose, while the Maenic put a grin on its face.

Before Krii had time to execute the helpless Emery, Rither charged at it. He poured all his power into the swing of his sword, hitting Krii's sword and knocking it out of its hand. Rither bashed again and again, each time hitting the raised shield and staggering back a step.

Krii dodged the sword, sending Rither stumbling past it. With a shield bash to his back, it knocked him to the floor. The Maenic retrieved its lost sword, and swung it around as it walked to Rither, who was still lying on the ground.

"You lose, Master Blade," it said with a smirk.

Emery's sword broke through the Maenic's belly, spattering its black blood all over. "No, you do!"

Looking at the sword sticking out of it, the smirk on Krii's face was wiped off and became a look of shock. Thick, black blood ran down its body and stained the dirty stone ground. Blood filled its mouth as it fell to its knees, pressing a hand against the wound.

It looked up at Rither as he rose to his feet. His angry face was the last thing it saw before everything turned black. Its head rolled away, leaving behind a thick trail of black blood. Emery grinned contently as blood dripped from his sword to the ground.

Behind them, Sizle and Tryden had succeeded in pushing back the soulless ones. Or had the abominations fled when the Maenic had been slain?

Rither stumbled up the pillar's staircase. He stared at the beautifully shiny crystal for a moment, and then swung his sword, abolishing the last crystal and breaking it into a million sparkling splinters.

Soon, Angus Kritz would be brought to justice; he would die for his crimes—his blasphemy.

8

The fire had long since died off. The soulless ones were nowhere to be seen. Both power crystals had been destroyed, and the energy field blocking the way down was gone. They could finally follow Angus Kritz, and kill him.

Rither feared the evil magic he sensed in the fort would be stronger below, perhaps strong enough to cause real harm. Still, they had no choice but to follow Kritz down; if Rynus Kalera was right, more was at stake than capturing an evil wizard—much more.

They were back on the platform in the vast room, staring into the depths of the spiral staircase. The darkness in the abyss was heavy and frightening, but they had to tread into it, no matter what. They moved downward, Sizle and Tryden at the vanguard, Emery and Adam in the middle, and Rither and Rynus at the rear.

"Halt, cursed mortals!" A dark, rough, and throaty voice came from behind. It was the darkest of the voices they had heard. "You can't go without saying 'hello', can you?"

Rither spun around. A Maenic stood at the top of the set of stairs, glaring down at them. It was even bigger, stronger, and more frightening than the other two. It wore the same kind of armor, but was unarmed.

"Gods damn it, another Maenic," Rither muttered. "Stay right there, demon! We have already slain two of you, and if you advance, we will have slain three!"

"I'm aware that you've killed my kin. I don't really care. If they are so weak they were slain by mere mortals, they'll be punished in Oblivion," the Maenic said with a grim face. "I, however, am much stronger than them. I am stronger than you. I am Od'kel."

Rither pushed the others gently down the stairs, keeping his eyes fixed on the Maenic—Od'kel. "You are no match for us either. We will kill you, and then stop whatever you and Angus Kritz are trying to achieve here."

"You mean stop us from bringing Oblivion into Siva? Even if you were to kill me, and I doubt you will, it is too late to stop us. Even if you stop us through some miracle, another plan has also been set in motion." Od'kel laughed smugly. "You are guardian blades, the guardians of Siva."

"What of it?" Rither retorted.

A grim grin appeared across the Maenic's face, turning its chiseled lines even darker. "Then our other scheme may be of interest to you. Have you heard of the Machine?"

"The Machine?" Rither thought of the Wall of Stories back at the Temple of the Precursors. They mentioned something about a machine—an apparatus of destruction—and seven keys that would power it.

"Yes. The Machine," Od'kel repeated, keeping the grin on its wretched face. "Like this fort—Fort Lockdown as you call it—it is the vanguard of your destruction."

"You lie!"

The Maenic bared its sharp teeth. "I do not! But it is of no consequence. If we succeed here, and believe you me, we'll succeed, the Machine won't be needed. Your days are numbered, filthy mortals."

Rither wrapped his hand tighter around his sword's hilt. "Enough! Let's get this over with!"

Od'kel closed its mouth, tightening its jaw. "That's fine by me. I will spare your souls the pain of watching your entire world burn. Consider it a gift."

It raised its arms well above its head, with the palms held toward each other. Black smoke appeared in between them. The smoke became a black orb, but didn't solidify; it looked as if a ball of black water hovered in the air, ripples spreading across it like waves. An aura of black smoke surrounded it, like clouds above a spherical ocean of darkness.

Rynus pushed Rither gently down the stairway. "It's using magic! I am better suited to battle it!" Rither stopped by the others a few steps down, looking up at Od'kel and Rynus.

The Maenic launched the orb of darkness toward Rynus. It soared through the air with a terrible speed. The very air it passed through was embedded with its dark magic. Rither could feel its power from where he stood.

Rynus put up both hands, as if getting ready to catch the dark sphere. His countenance was unreadable. His eyes were blank. Even though he could not see it, Rither could swear Rynus had an aura about him.

The black mass flew into Rynus, exploding in a powerful whirlwind of dark magic. It sent a wave of pain through the men. Smoke filled the staircase. Od'kel's manic laughter cut through it, pounding at Rither's ears.

Fear captured Rither; he did not know if he could combat Od'kel's sheer power. He feared Rynus had been killed, that the wizard was not powerful enough either. If that were the case, all would be lost.

As the smoke subsided, a blue shimmer freed itself. The light highlighted the dark shape of Rynus. When the smoke was gone, Rither could see him standing there with a sphere of blue light between his hands, similar to what Angus Kritz had used. Flashes of electricity jumped from one side of the sphere to another.

Rynus sent his magic flying toward Od'kel. It soared onward with a terrible speed, like Od'kel's dark magic. The air it passed through was embedded with lighter, kinder magic, deadly but not as terrifying—at least not to Rither.

Od'kel raised its hands, just like Rynus had done. Instead of the magic exploding when it reached the demon, Od'kel caught it and sent it flying upward, into the darkness of the enormous room above. It did not take long before the magic had disappeared in the emptiness, faint flashes of electricity being all that remained.

Od'kel and Rynus glared at one another with blank concentration, without blinking. Their countenances flickered with loathing for each other. It was as if they could see only each other; no one and nothing else existed for them; they were sealed away from the world, inside their magic.

Once again, Od'kel charged a ball of darkness and Rynus an orb of light. The magic increased in power by the second. The calm before the storm was unsettling. Rither could feel a tingle of excitement in his body. The ground beneath his feet trembled with the power of magic.

They sent the orbs of magic flying through the air toward the other. The spells collided in midair. The dark and light absorbed each other; the magic vanished. All sound disappeared. The deafening silence weighed heavy on them.

All sound returned. The magic—the light and dark—came back, swirling about in a vortex. It expanded with lightning speed, sending a powerful force wave slamming into everything it came across. Od'kel was thrown from the stairs. The men tumbled into the dark madness. Walls came crumbling down; smoke and debris filled the staircase.

When the dust had settled, Rither, Emery, Tryden, Sizle, Rynus, and Adam lay at the bottom of the stairs, knocked about, but alive. The stairway up was completely blocked off by a wall of debris; they had nowhere to go but forward, into the unknown.

The hallway ahead was shrouded in utter darkness; they could not see a thing. Still, Rither had the feeling something was there, something ominous. He had long since learned to trust his gut feeling.

A growl sounded from the shroud of shadows. The ground shook as whatever was there slowly moved forward. Two red dots—glowing eyes—appeared down the passage, five leaps above the floor. With a gleam of hunger, they were fixed on their prey.

Looking into them was like looking into malice; it was like looking into the fiery depths of Oblivion itself...

TAH ANSENTA MAS'PLU

1

Soft footsteps echoed through the vast darkness of the corridor ahead. The area had a complete and utter absence of light. The man had the same feeling as always when walking through the hallway; it felt like pacing through absolute emptiness. He knew it was not so; one wrong step and he'd smack into the wall. Had he not known the place so well, he would have flattened his nose many times.

In the distance, he heard a muffled roar; the baldran had awoken. The guardian blades had beaten the challenge he had given to them. They had proved themselves to be worthy adversaries. He would destroy them, and he could take pride in that.

Something unnerved him; he sensed one more presence. Rynus Kalera had been let out of his cage. But he would die with the rest of them. He was merely another soul to feed to the fire.

The man reached his destination. A room opened up before him, a few dozen leaps broad, but reaching tileaps into the darkness ahead, up, and down. It consisted of multiple levels of walkways lining the walls, with hundreds of closed and locked prison cells.

He waved his arm across the room, proclaiming in an ancient language, "Agema vani, kraeturi af evaeni agum, ae nu relaas dae. Nu don mae viljae. Devaaren bladeni."

Countless of red dots flashed into existence, in every cell. They were the lights that would bring forth darkness. They were the shadows that would blacken out the sun.

The ancient ones had awoken.

2

A shiver ran down Rither Pleagau's spine, and his neck hair stood up. He didn't know if it was because of the creature in front of him or something else, but for the moment, his coin was on the beast.

It was still hidden in utter darkness, its red-glowing eyes standing out like an aevir amidst men. Rither got the sense the creature was massive; its hungry eyes were suspended a few leaps up, and its sense of power was intense.

"What do you think that is?" Sizle stammered. "You don't suppose it's a dragon—a real dragon—do you?"

"Don't be silly, Brother Sizle," Tryden replied, as calmly as his voice would let him. "Dragons are extinct; they were all slain by the dragon hunters of old."

"Maybe there are some left, hiding in the darkness of forts and mountains."

"Nothing is ever easy, is it?" Rither muttered. In hopes the magic counteracting his silk veil's invisibility was gone, he said, "Invaesen aktivaae," but to no avail.

"No good, boss," Emery grunted. "I say we kill it."

"I'd say it's more likely going to kill us," Sizle stuttered.

"Don't be such a pessimist and coward, Brother Sizle."

"He is not a coward, Brother Emery," Tryden said. "Being frightened doesn't make you a coward. In fact, without fear, is there really bravery?"

"Spoken like a true scholar and warrior," Rither stated. "It never hurts to be afraid. Foolish arrogance gets you killed. It will do you well to remember this, Brother Emery."

Torches lit up all along the corridor, casting an eerie, blue light. Basking in their cold glow was the beast. It looked so horrendous Rither wished the torches had stayed unlit.

The beast was—like he had measured—of immense size; it was five leaps tall and three leaps broad. It had an angled posture, and walked on two hind legs, but used its massive arms to hold itself up. Rither reckoned it could only lift one at a time, lest lose its footing.

Its head was big, round, and as ugly as a face could be. It had an ugly, flat nose with mucus and a mouth with rotten, uneven teeth. Its rough skin was greenish and grayish, with warts, deformations, and scars from a violent life. Its ragged clothes barely covered its huge muscles and privates.

"It looks a little bit like you, Brother Emery," Tryden joked with a nervous laugh. "Don't you think?"

"Very funny," Emery said, with a clear lack of laughter. "It probably thinks you're laughing at it. It will eat you first for that. The rest of us can escape while it's busy with you."

"The baldran," Rynus mumbled.

"Not one of these freaks," Rither muttered.

"You've run into a baldran before?"

"And I wished I'd never have to again. I ran for two hours with it chasing me. They're slow, but tenacious."

"We have nowhere to run; we must fight it. My magic and your steel may bring it down."

Rither met the baldran's glowing eyes. They terrified him; the baldran he met before had eyes as cold as the night, but this baldran was like an embodiment of Oblivion.

The baldran started moving toward them. Its massive size and posture didn't allow it to move too quickly. But it didn't need to be quick; it had a wide reach, and one slap could be enough to kill.

"Sizle, could you take care of Adam?" Rynus requested.

"What about the baldran?" It was apparent that Sizle was afraid, but he didn't want to abandon his blade brothers.

"Someone has to take care of Adam, make sure he's safe. My magic will be important in the coming battle."

Sizle looked from Rynus to his master.

Rither gave him a nod. "Take care of Adam. We'll be fine."

Anthony Sizle backed away with an arm wrapped around Adam Kalera. The other blades and the wizard stood ready to combat the great beast.

The baldran swiped its huge arm in an arc, forcing them back. Rither cut deep into the beast's arm. It staggered back in pain, before advancing once again. It seemed he had done nothing but stagger it for a moment.

Rynus held out his arms. His hands had a gentle, blue glow about them—a mist of magic. The glow appeared about the baldran, which froze in its current movement.

"Kill it!" the wizard bellowed. "I can't hold it forever!"

The blades approached the baldran carefully, unknowing whether or not Rynus's spell would hold. The beast did not move, so it appeared to be working. Sword after sword hit it. Blood flooded onto the floor as the baldran wailed.

Its magical nature and strong will to kill broke the spell. Rynus yelped as the aura became red. He quieted and wrinkled his face, concentrating deeply. His countenance eased as the aura disappeared.

The baldran swiped its arms sideways, forcing the blades backward, and then staggered away. Its pain was as severe as Rynus's. It had been hurt greatly. It roared into the stale air, and started thrashing with its giant arms and stomping with its giant feet. It was going mad.

The passage shook. Pebbles came loose as a crack spread across the ceiling. Dust spread out like a cloud. With a loud crash, a big boulder came down, just missing Rither.

He staggered back, and shouted over the immense sound of rocks crashing down, "We've got to get out of here!"

Tryden nodded concurringly. Emery just stared at Rither, not even a flicker of emotion in his countenance. Sizle could not hide his fear, but without hesitating moved to the others with Adam under his arm.

In an attempt to give them an opportunity to get past the raging baldran, Rynus Kalera sent a burst of fire at it. The flames enveloped the baldran, staggering it into the wall.

"Now, let's go!" the wizard shouted.

They took off through the chaos of dust and rocks falling down. Several times, rocks almost crushed them, squished the life out of them with their insides. They made it past the baldran, onward through the blue-lit hallway.

The passage shook worse than before; it felt like the world was shaking. The fire around the baldran disappeared, and it came after them. It wanted its kill; it needed the death.

Rither ducked as the giant fist came for him. It struck the wall instead, and cracks spread outward. If this continued, the ceiling would come down on top of their heads.

"There's a narrower passage up ahead!" Tryden bellowed. "Too small for the freak!"

Rither looked ahead, seeing the narrower hallway. If they could make it into it, the baldran wouldn't be able to follow. "Run for your lives! Pray that Athra watches over us!"

He looked to Sizle and Adam. They were having a difficult time keeping up a quick pace. The baldran was right behind them, its demonic eyes fixed on them. While it was slow, it could easily catch up to them.

Rither rushed back. He wouldn't leave them behind, even if it killed him.

The baldran lunged for its prey. Its fist broke through the air, bringing forceful death with it. Death would catch Sizle and Adam; they would be reduced to pulp.

Rither jumped in, sword first. He cut into the beast's fist, spattering its blood to the wall and floor. The baldran stumbled away, wailing in pain. Rither and Sizle grabbed Adam, and dragged him to the safety the others had reached.

The baldran had not given up yet; with everything coming down, it charged after the three men. Its ugly features were twisted in vile anger. The only thought in its tiny mind was to bring death.

The great beast swung one of its colossal arms at its prey. Rither took a tight grip of both Adam and Sizle, and dragged them with him, onto the floor in the narrower hallway. The fist missed them, and hit the wall instead.

Everything stood still for a moment. Silence settled upon the area. The ceiling of the broader passageway came down with a thunderous roar. Rither could not perceive anything through the dust, except a wail amid the ruckus. When the dust settled, his eyes met a wall of rocks.

The way back was blocked off.

3

"But what if we can't fucking get back out!?"

"Calm down, little man," Emery said.

"Calm down!?" Sizle responded. "How can I fucking calm down!? We're blocked in! The whole passage caved in! We'll never dig through it! We'll never get out! We'll never see the sun again!"

"And freaking out will do any good?"

Sizle opened his mouth, but closed it right afterward. Instead, he sank down against the wall, staring blindly at the blackness in front of him.

Leaning in toward Rither, Emery cleared his throat softly. "Boss, he's got a point, though; not about the rambling, we-ain't-never-gonna-see-the-sun-again crap, but we're stuck in here. Any ideas?"

Rither nodded. "We move on. We kill Kritz."

Tryden leaned in, too. "I examined Adam. He is not doing well; he is feverish and pale. It is too quick for an infection. I don't know what the hell is going on. It's perplexing."

Rither nodded. "Thanks for telling me, but we can't worry about that now. Kritz has priority, even if we should all die. As long as he goes down, we're expendable."

Tryden faced Sizle, Rynus, and Adam. "Get on your feet, everyone. Let's kill Kritz, and then worry about a way out." He smiled at Sizle. "Don't worry, Anthony. Vast forts usually have more than one exit."

Sizle rose to his feet, rubbing his eyes. "I'm sorry. I didn't mean to freak out."

With Rither taking the lead, they moved the only way they could—deeper into the fort, through the narrow hallway. It continued onward forever, seemingly never ending. Torches didn't light up, so they kept close to Rynus, who had set his hand aflame with magic.

"For how long have the Guardian Blades been after Kritz?" Rynus wondered, glancing at Rither. "Weeks? Months?"

Rither shook his head. "Years."

"How come you haven't caught him yet?"

"He is a slippery bastard. I was on his trail ten years ago, but I lost it. Then he vanished, like a ghost. I found his trail again mere months ago."

"What happened ten years ago?" Sizle asked.

Rither glanced at him, and then at Tryden and Emery. "It was before either of you joined the Guardian Blades of Siva. I hadn't even become a blade master yet. However, this is of no importance."

"Why not? I'd like to hear it. Besides, it appears we have a long walk ahead of us."

Rither sighed. "Ten years ago, we got disturbing news; we heard of people—communities—vanishing. They were all in eastern Cyra, the outskirts of the civilized world. Numerous squads were sent out to learn why this was occurring.

"I was the leader of one such squad. Back then, it was not common practice for the master blades to be out in the field, like I am. At any rate, we followed a trail of... well, vacancy. We came to village after village, finding all empty. We didn't know what the hell was going on.

"The trail finally led us to Tauni, a region in eastern Cyra that is enclosed by mountains in pretty much all directions. Not many people live there, and few know how to get there. We had to have an old man living in the vicinity lead us into the region, through a mountain pass.

"Once there, we made our way to the first of two villages. It was empty, like all other villages we had been to. Also like the other villages, we found a platform and altar of rock and burnt-out candles.

"When we were a few hundred leaps away from the other village, I could hear a voice, like it drifted on the wind without fading. I heard a man proclaim he was Angus Kritz and was doing the work of the True God—Drahc Uhr.

"When we finally got there, I saw—" Rither sighed. "I was too late. The villagers had been herded like cattle to the center of the village. They sat crouched down around a platform and altar. Masked warriors like the ones we killed when we entered this Gods-forsaken fort guarded them like dogs.

"On the platform, I saw a hooded man, a masked warrior, a woman restrained by the warrior, and a little girl, who lay on the altar. The hooded man, Kritz, held a dagger over the girl. Her father burst out of a house. He killed two masked warriors, before one hit him in his back with the butt of the sword. They beat him, kicked at his face.

"I had little time to act. I ran for Kritz and the little girl as fast as I could, but I did not even make it halfway before the dagger fell."

Rither fell silent, letting his words sink in. Silence rang in their ears. They were dazed, gawking silently at Rither. Sizle dared not speak. Rynus gave more attention to his hurt and sick cousin than the story.

Rither pulled a hand through his thick beard. "I won't go into the specifics of that horror. Suffice it to say that it was the most horrifying, cruel act I've ever witnessed. There's no doubt in my mind that Angus Kritz should burn in Oblivion. Men have done horrible things in the past, but Kritz... He is not human; he is a monster."

Sizle swallowed. "So he just killed a little girl?"

"No, he didn't just kill her. He sacrificed her to summon a Maenic."

Rynus turned from his cousin to Rither, with his mouth and eyes wide open. "Kritz sacrificed a human being to soul-summon a Maenic?"

With a glance at Rynus, Rither nodded. "I ran my sword through the Maenic, before it could cause trouble. Kritz got away. He took the mother of the young girl with him. I have never forgiven myself for that, for arriving too late."

"Dear Althir," Rynus whispered, "forgive me."

"Forgive you?" Tryden asked. "Forgive you for what?"

"A couple weeks ago, Kritz sent me on a mission. I was to capture three evildoers. I did. I brought them to Kritz. Now I think... Maybe they weren't evildoers. Maybe—"

"Maybe Angus Kritz used them to soul-summon the three Maenics, J'da, Krii, and Od'kel?" Tryden finished.

Emery spun around and moved to Rynus. He wrapped his

hands in the wizard's robes, and slammed him against the wall. "You did what!?"

Rither spun around, too. "Emery, stop! Release him!"

"Boss, he took three innocent people!" Emery said. "Three people who Kritz sacrificed to summon Maenics!"

"Be that as it may, he did not know, and we may yet have need of him. Now let him go. You owe me."

Emery met Rynus's eyes, gritting his teeth and growling. A second later, he pushed him away and turned from him. "Fine! But I don't have to like it."

4

They had walked through the nothingness for an eternity, it seemed, but something finally met their eyes. It was a room, lit by blue-burning torches. On the left and right, passages led out of the room. Rither's attention got caught on the wall straight ahead.

The wall was covered in writing. He knew the language. It was Thalman, which bifurcated to Imperial and Aeviri after man left Eural in search of new lands—the Dragonlands. It was thousands of years old.

"Ah, there you are, dear guardian blades, at last," a voice proclaimed. "And my disciple and his imbecile cousin."

Angus Kritz came forth from a shadowed corner. Rither's gaze immediately went to the white and black eyes, but then took in the rest of Kritz's wretched, aged face.

Rither's sword came out of the scabbard on his back, and the other blades drew theirs, too. Without a moment's hesitation, they charged at the wicked wizard. A ball of fire flew past them, having been chucked by Rynus.

The old man did nothing; he just smiled. The fire collided with him and enveloped him. Rither swung his sword at the man-shaped fire, but was stopped. The fire exploded, hurling the blades to Rynus and Adam. Kritz appeared between the flames, and waved his hand so everyone froze up.

"Good try, dear blades and Rynus," Kritz panted, resting

against the wall with inscriptions, "but not good enough."

"If you're gonna kill us, just get it over with," Emery said, trying to break free. "You're too cowardly to fight."

"If I could kill you, I would. Magic takes concentration; I cannot kill you and keep up the spell to paralyze you at the same time. I hate to admit it, but with Rynus you might just have the advantage—at least here."

Rither snorted. "Then what do you want!?"

"I've got a second challenge for you, Master Blade," Kritz answered. "But first, let me tell you something."

"Just tell us the challenge!"

"This fort was not always called Fort Lockdown. At first, it was called Gateway Keep, when the dragons reigned."

"Why was it called that?" Tryden asked. "And why was its name changed?"

"That, I won't say," Kritz mocked them. "What I can say is that prisoners were kept here. They were executed."

"Executed!?" Sizle inquired. "For what!?"

"They were rebels against the children of Lord Uhr."

"You mean dragons," Tryden stated, more than asked.

"According to legend, they killed the prisoners by breathing their magic fire on them. I honestly cannot imagine how painful that must have been."

"And still you're aligned with them!?" Rither shouted.

"I said their fire hurts. I did not say they're evil. It was we mortals who drove them away. They had to retaliate."

"They enslaved us! How can you be on their side, knowing that!?"

"How can citizens of a kingdom accept their king for no reason other than the fact he was born? It is their birthright to rule! They are the children of the True God!"

"An evil god!"

Kritz sighed. "How blind you are. I cannot convince you of the truth. But I digress. The challenge! I'll descend yet another floor. You'll have to follow me. Look ahead to find the way below."

Kritz's magic vanished and they were released from their paralyses. Before they could act, Kritz raised his arms high and bright light shone from them. Rither could not see; his eyes were filled with the blinding light.

When it faded and the room became dark, Kritz was gone. All Rither saw was the wall with inscriptions. He blinked in surprise, also trying to get rid of the rainbow-colored spots floating before his eyes. Where had the old wizard gone?

5

"So why is this place called Fort Lockdown, anyways?" Sizle asked, casting a quick glance to Rither studying the text on the wall, and then returning his gaze to Tryden.

Tryden shrugged, without removing his gaze from Rither's back. He didn't know the answer.

"Rumor has it they used to lock down violent criminals in the depths of this fort," Rynus Kalera answered in his place. "Rumor has it that those criminals are still here, longing to let loose their vengeance on the next innocent soul they see. I guess it is true. Kritz pretty much told us so, didn't he?"

"Yeah, maybe, but the prisoners he spoke of were imprisoned here when this place was called Gateway Keep," Sizle argued. "You know, when the dragons reigned."

Tryden nodded concurringly, still not looking away from Rither. "Perhaps there is another reason why it's called Fort Lockdown."

Rither turned to the others, clearing his throat. "The text on the wall is in Thalman. Lucky for us, I can read it."

Emery crossed his arms. "So what does it say, boss?"

"It reads, 'Hirae lajen port til verlen af faer. Tsa uphaar nedlas, sprecken verti af maenicae magikae til hajgar ock vanstar'," Rither read aloud.

Emery just looked at him with his arms still crossed, and Tryden raised his eyebrows. Then Sizle asked what all were thinking. "What the hell does that mean?"

"It means, 'Here lies the doorway to the world of fire. To cease the lockdown, speak the words of unholy magic to the right and left'," Rither translated.

"What lockdown? And what about 'words to the right and left'? What does that mean?"

"I don't know. I see no other words here."

"Maybe there are more words somewhere to the literal left and right," Tryden suggested. He gestured to the doorways at the sides of the room. "One passage in each direction. I'd bet we'll find more words there."

"That could be what the text means," Rither agreed. "Say, Brother Tryden, do you know any Thalman?"

"I cannot speak it, no. I know no words, but I do know the Thalmanian alphabet, so I should be able to read it, though I won't know what it means."

"Take Emery with you to the right. Sizle and I will go left," Rither said, with a contented smile on his lips. "Divide and conquer. Remember the words, should you find any."

Tryden nodded, and patted Emery twice on the shoulder. "Yes, Master Pleagau. We'll leave presently."

Rither watched Tryden and Emery disappear into the corridor to the right. He turned to Sizle. "Are you ready?"

"I am, Master," Sizle said with a nervous smile.

Rither turned to Rynus, merely glancing at the pale and sweaty Adam. "And you'll be fine here with Adam?"

The young gifted one gave his cousin a concerned glance, and then nodded. "We'll be fine. Go get the words needed to unlock the doorway to the world of fire, whatever that is."

Rither already had a suspicion of what it was, and Rynus probably had one, too, but did not want to admit it to himself. Rither didn't either; it frightened him too much.

With a final glance at the passageway Tryden and Emery had disappeared into, Rither turned to the one on the other side of the room. He sensed powerful magic in its depths. It scared him almost as much as what he thought they would find beyond the doorway did.

The Gods knew how he hated magic.

6

Rither headed into the dark, trailed by Sizle. A few leaps in, a torch burning with a warm, orange glow hung on the wall. Beyond it followed only darkness.

He stopped by the torch. It felt so out of character in the vileness of Fort Lockdown. Turning to the darkness ahead, he glanced at the torch. He wrapped his hand around it and yanked it free. It came loose easily.

With the torch in hand, Rither led Sizle into the passage. Like he suspected, no torches lit up. The only source of light was the one in his hand, and its light was swallowed by the blackness too quickly.

"What do you make of all this, Master?" Sizle asked him.

"Of all what?" Rither wondered.

"Maenics. Bringing Oblivion to Siva. All that scary shit."

Rither glanced at Sizle. He was obviously afraid. "I do not know what to make of it. It should not be possible to bring Oblivion into Siva, but the Maenics, Angus Kritz, and Rynus have all spoken of it."

"Yeah. Maybe they're all lying, though."

"That's a possibility, but nonetheless, it is our job to find out if there's any truth to their words, and if there is, stop it from happening."

As they continued in silence, Rither tried to examine their surroundings, but merely saw blackness. Soon, the corridor opened up into a vast room. It reached into the unseen up, down, and forward. It consisted of multiple levels, lined with hundreds of prison cells.

Rither and Sizle were on a secluded ledge overlooking the massive room. Two passageways led from the ledge. One led to a stairway to the prison. The other led to the unknown.

"Where do you think the wall with words we're looking for is?" Sizle asked, looking into the vast room.

"Probably not in the prison," Rither muttered. "Let's head the other way."

With a nod, Sizle headed to the doorway to the unknown.

Rither started for it, too, but stopped; he thought he had seen something. His eyes darted from one corner of the vast room to the next. He saw nothing, and after a few moments and a nudge from Sizle, he decided it was nothing.

Leaving, he didn't notice the countless flashes of red, like light bouncing off a hundred tiny rubies.

"This place is crazy," Sizle said. "It's massive, much larger than it looked from the outside."

Rither did not answer; he had predicted the fort would be incredibly vast. He focused on not slipping, making his way down a narrow, spiraling staircase. It flattened to a hallway much too broad for his torchlight to reach from wall to wall. To make sure there were no branching pathways, he had to zigzag from wall to wall.

Nearing the walls, Rither thought he could see things, but reaching them, he saw nothing but dark-gray stone. Tricks of the mind, he reasoned. What else could it be? What could be hiding in the dark?

A thud caused his heart to jump into his throat. He spun around, drawing his sword. His heart dropped into a pit in his stomach; Sizle was nowhere to be seen.

"Anthony!" he called out. "Anthony, where are you!?"

"Master Pleagau!" Sizle called back. "I'm over here!"

Rither sprinted back. Almost right away, Sizle came into view. He was lying on the ground with an impish grin on his face. Rither gave him a sharp look.

"Sorry, I tripped," Sizle said. "Help me up?"

Rither rolled his eyes, sheathed his sword, and helped the young blade up. "Damn it, Sizle, you gave me a scare."

"I suspected as much when you called me Anthony," Sizle said with a grin on his childish face. "I'm okay, though."

Rither did not return the smile. He turned away instead, and headed onward again. Sizle quickly caught up, wanting to be in the circle of light provided by the torch. He was just as frightened as Rither, and probably even more so.

They were scared with good reason; with the magic in the fort—heavier farther into the depths—anything could reside there. Many vile creatures thrived in magic, and others produced it. At times, Rither got the impression that magic was inherently malicious, but that was fortunately not the case. In actuality, magic was power, a force of corruption.

Sizle's footsteps echoed loudly. Each one tore through the moist silence like a knife through butter. Rither wished they had their silk veils to safeguard them, but they did not; they were as visible as Sizle was loud. If anything was hiding in a corner, it knew exactly where they were.

They encountered a dead end straight forward. To the left, a doorway led to a set of stairs delving even farther into Fort Lockdown's depths. Rither took a couple of steps down, but stopped when he didn't hear Sizle follow.

He spun around, facing the young blade at the top of the stairway. "Sizle, what is it? Why did you stop?"

Sizle stood with his side to Rither, looking to the shadows whence they had come. "I don't know. I just had a feeling."

"A feeling?"

Sizle glanced at Rither. "I think something is here."

Rither was about to reply when a scuffing sound made its way toward them. Instead, he moved his hand to the hilt of his sword. Sizle was way ahead of him; he had moved forth, with a drawn sword. Rither heard his footsteps echo off into the distance, but then they stopped.

"What's going on, Sizle!?" Rither called out. "Anthony, are you okay!?"

"Oh, dear Gods!" Sizle stumbled out of the dark, running toward the stairway.

"Sizle, stop!" Rither commanded.

He didn't stop. He crashed into Rither, and they tumbled down. Rither's back hit the stairs hard, Sizle on top of him, and they rolled over, time and time again, until they hit the floor below. Everything was spinning. He felt nauseated and woozy. He tried to focus on the light a few leaps away—his torch, which he had dropped in the fall.

He pressed a hand against his throbbing side. "What the hell, Sizle!"

"Sorry, Master," Sizle groaned. "I saw... something."

"Then kill it next time! Don't run into me!"

"But, sir, you don't know what I saw!"

Rither looked up the stairs. Merely darkness met his eyes. "Nothing's there, Brother Sizle."

Sizle looked up the staircase, too, seeing the nothingness, and then let his head fall back down to the ground. "Sorry, Master Pleagau."

Rither rose up, and held out his hand. "Don't worry about it, young blade. But try not to do it again."

Sizle grasped the hand, and Rither pulled him to his feet. They looked up the stairway again, and then at each other. Rither headed through the narrow hallway they now found themselves in, retrieving the torch when he passed it.

Up ahead, the passage ended in light. With a tight grip of his sword's hilt, he made his way there. He entered a grand room, lit with warm, orange-burning torches. He took in the peculiarity of the warm glow in this vile place.

His eyes wandered to the rest of the room. It was circular, and had a high ceiling. Carved into the sand-colored walls and ceiling were dragons, humans, aevira, and Thalmanian words. There was also something else.

Rither's stare settled on a carving in the ceiling. It was of the same mystical figure they had seen at the beginning of Fort Lockdown. It was impossible to make out what it was, but its eyes were two rubies, jammed into the rock ceiling. It felt as if the rubies glared at him, following him.

"Beware the ancient ones," Rither mumbled.

He tore his gaze off of the unnerving figure, and turned to what was straight ahead. At the room's far end, three steps led to a raised platform shaped as a half circle. He walked to it, and took the three steps up.

He headed straight across, to the wall, which was slightly rounded with words inscribed into it. Sizle caught up, and placed himself next to Rither, staring at the words in awe.

"I think we've found what we are looking for," Rither said, with a contented smile. "Wouldn't you say?"

"Yeah," Sizle agreed. "What's it say?"

Rither read the words on the wall aloud. "Enaean vii stett

maat maenicae. It means—"

The torches went out all at once, including the one in his hand. Rither could not even see his own hand. With a thud, he felt Sizle walk into him. Yet another thud echoed through the compressing darkness, near the room's exit.

Rither and Sizle froze up, pressed up against each other. Rither could feel the beating of both their hearts. The words he had read echoed through his mind, over and over.

Enaean vii stett maat maenicae.

He took Sizle's arm, and dragged him along. They moved down the three steps, and treaded through the room. Before getting even halfway, the stroll was cut short. Countless red dots flashed into existence all around them, leaving no way out; pairwise, they came to be at an alarming pace.

A scuffing sound broke the silence, otherwise broken by Sizle's labored breathing. As the outline of something moved toward them from the blackness ahead, Rither saw the unnerving figure in his mind's eye.

With the scuffing closing in and Rither getting used to the dark, more of the silhouette became visible. His eyes went to the red strip of cloth first. It was draped around the neck of a man, and reached down the middle of the body to over the knees. A belt around the waist held the cloth in place.

His eyes continued to the sides of the cloth. They took in the pasty, wrinkled skin there, which stuck too close to the bone. The man was so thin all his bones were clearly visible, even in the low light. All fluids seemed to have been drained from him, leaving him a dried-up husk.

Rither's stare moved to the face. The red-glowing eyes met his. When they did, the light died off, revealing a pair of eyes glazed white. They looked dead, but still they did not.

The man shrieked, his wrinkled, dead features twisting in a horrifying way. The other ruby eyes all flashed bright red, before dying off. The scuffing resumed from every direction. Silhouettes of humans became perceivable in the dark.

But they were not human—not any longer. They were the ancient ones.

7

Tryden glanced around the corner, seeing nothing there. He rounded it, with the warm flame of his torch held out and a sword secured in his left hand.

Emery followed close behind, not paying a single thought to what could be hiding behind any corners. His sword was in his hand. If anything came for him, he was ready to cut it into pieces.

They had moved through a hallway for a half hour, taking turn after turn. They were lucky it had no branching paths. Tryden had long ago lost track of the direction in which they were heading. With all these turns and long passages thereafter, they might as well have been on the same side of the room where they had split up as Rither and Sizle were.

Looking around another corner, Tryden headed onward. He thanked the Gods for watching over them; no vile beasts had bothered them. He had feared that soulless ones, clavi, or clav would do so, but they hadn't. Other than Tryden and Emery, the area was devoid of life.

After rounding another corner, Tryden came to a stop. He saw light up ahead. He gave Emery a wondering look, which was returned with a blank stare, and then headed for it.

They came to an amazingly humongous room. It stretched far to the left, right, up, and down, but was only a few dozen leaps across. The room's several levels were lined with cells. Tryden and Emery were on a secluded walkway, which led across the room between two levels.

"What do you suppose was locked away in here?" Tryden wondered. "The rebels against the dragons?"

"Who cares, Brother Tryden?" Emery muttered.

"I care, Brother Emery."

"Fine! Yes, probably the rebels. Can we move on now?"

Tryden nodded once, and they headed across the narrow bridge. No railings shielded them from the drop to nothingness below. If they fell, they would surely die.

Looking around the area, Tryden shuddered; he could see levels lined with cells as far as the faint light allowed. Thousands had been kept here, all executed by dragon fire. What had happened to them since? Had the fire evaporated them? Had they been buried in a mass grave? Had they been left to rot where they had died?

On the bridge's other side, they moved through a doorway leading into another corridor with twists and turns. Tryden wished they would just find the words, so they could follow Kritz. He wanted to kill that bastard, for what he was trying to do here and for what he had done in the past.

"I never said I'm sorry for what happened to you," he said, looking to Emery's dark shape behind him.

Emery stopped and closed his eyes. "Come on, please not this. Not now."

Tryden stopped, turning fully to the Emery. "But, Emery, I—"

"I don't wanna hear it."

"Why not!? Do you hate me that much!?"

Emery looked away, with a heavy sigh, before once again facing Tryden. "I don't hate you. I just—"

"What!? What then!?"

Emery shut his eyes again, and Tryden thought he could see the hint of a tear, even though Emery was a shadow. "I never let myself think of it, okay!?"

Silence. "Oh, I didn't realize. I'm so sorry, Emery."

Emery shook away the tears. "Don't worry. I'm fine."

Tryden gawked in silence, before deciding it was best not to say anything. He turned away from Emery and continued through the corridor. He had never realized how much pain Emery held on to.

"I'm sorry, Tryden," Emery said. "I appreciate your sentiment. You're a good friend."

Tryden didn't look back. He didn't stop. He didn't speak. He just nodded. He could scarcely grasp the concept; Emery had called him his friend.

Now in silence, the two blades followed the corridor to its end. They found a narrow staircase leading up. Exchanging glances once, they headed up to a passage ending in a wall of light. Had they reached their destination?

A sound coming from down the stairs caught Tryden's ear. He spun around, seeing it had caught Emery's attention, as well. "What do you suppose it is?"

Emery shrugged. "I don't know. Ain't nothing good in this place."

"Agreed. Should we investigate, or move on ahead?"

Emery didn't answer. Instead, he started down the stairs. Tryden followed, letting the light of his torch wash over their surrounds. Step by step, they headed down.

"I don't see anything," Tryden whispered.

"Shh. Be quiet," Emery told him.

They stood silent, looking into the dark. Tryden could feel his heart pound in his chest; he felt the fear it pumped out. He wanted his silk veil to guard him. This was the first time he was without it.

A scuffing sound returned him to reality. Something was heading toward them. Tryden fingered his sword's hilt, while Emery boldly stared ahead. Both waited to engage what was coming. They would slay whatever vile thing was there. But then the scuffing ceased a couple leaps away; silence fell on their ears again.

"Come," Emery said, and headed to where the sound had come from.

Hesitantly, Tryden followed him, with torch and sword in hand. Slowly, they moved one step after the other. The spot where the sound had come from was a pace away.

Torchlight washed over the area. Tryden held his breath, and tried listening to his surrounds despite the loud beating of his heart. The spot was empty; all he saw was the stone floor. He let out a deep breath, and calmed himself.

A jolt of fear ran through him; he saw a human with his peripheral vision. Looking there, he saw no one; only he and Emery were there.

"What?" Emery wondered.

"I thought I saw something," Tryden muttered. "I guess it was nothing."

"What was it you saw?"

"I thought I saw"—Tryden turned to see if anyone was behind them—"someone, but no one's here but us."

"The mind can play tricks on us in the dark. Ain't nothing to be ashamed of."

"Yeah," Tryden muttered.

"Let's keep going instead. We're almost there."

"Let's hope so. Let's hope it was only a trick by my mind, conjured by the Lord of Darkness, Shrada."

They headed up the staircase again, Tryden up front and Emery behind him. They treaded through the final corridor, to the light at its end. Reaching it, they came into a circular room. Etched into its high ceiling and walls were words and depictions.

Tryden's eyes were drawn to the sinister, humanoid figure carved into the ceiling. It was the same as the one Sizle had pointed out to them at the very beginning of the fort. It was the one under which the text 'Beware the ancient ones' had been written in Aeviri, by whom, they didn't know.

Tryden was glad the room was lit up with orange-burning torches. The sand-colored stone the room was made of was much warmer in tone than the dark-gray stone making up the rest of the fort. At the far side, a three-steps-high platform sported a wall with Thalmanian words. They were the words they were looking for; they had to be.

Tryden marched straight to the Thalmanian words, while Emery pranced about, studying the multiple inscriptions on the walls and ceiling. The former blade made his way up the three steps, and then to the wall with the words.

"Can you read it!?" Emery called from a bit away.

"I think so, yeah!" Tryden called back.

"Let's hear it, brother bookworm!"

It was long since he studied Thalman, or used it for that matter. "Let's see. I think it says... Wait. That's that symbol. Right. And if that is that symbol, then it must say—"

"Well!?"

"Don't rush me," Tryden said with a mutter. "Yes! I've got it! It says, 'ock iatil faer vii skael gaht'!"

Emery came up behind him. "Any idea what it means?"

Tryden glanced at him. "Not even almost. As I told Master Pleagau, I know the Thalmanian alphabet, but I can't speak or understand the language."

"Then ain't it a waste knowing the alphabet?"

"Evidently it isn't. I know what it says, not what it means. We could split up and cut the time this would take in half. Even if neither I nor Master Pleagau understood the words, we'd still be able to speak them and open the gateway."

"Sure, but boss would not have been able to translate the first set of writing, which let us know what to do."

"True, but it still isn't a waste."

"Fine!" Emery yelled, turning his back to Tryden. "It ain't a waste."

When he finished the sentence and Tryden was about to retort, all the lights in the room went out, including the fire of the torch Tryden held; it was as if someone blinded them by pulling a giant sheet over them.

"What the fuck," Emery said.

"What happened?" Tryden wondered.

"I don't know, but we're getting the hell out of here before we find out. Come on!"

Emery grabbed Tryden's arm, and pulled him through the room, their hasty footsteps echoing. It was hard to find their way in the darkness; they couldn't see anything at all.

No, that was not true; red dots of light broke free from the blackness. They were everywhere. A scuffing sound between them and the exit caught their attention.

Emery didn't stop. He pulled Tryden toward the sound. A creature appeared. It was a human, but its skin was pasty and wrinkled, and the bones were visible through it. A piece of cloth covered the center of its body, wrapped around the neck and hanging down to just above the knees. A belt held it in place by the waist.

Tryden looked at the human's face. It was disgusting and grotesque, with pasty, wrinkled skin, yellow teeth, and red-glowing eyes. Even Emery could not help skidding to a halt and staring at it.

The light in the eyes died off. The eyes were glazed white. They looked dead, but something was off about them; there was a spark of darkness in them.

The creature screeched, and the ruby eyes all around the room flashed bright red before dying away. Tryden assumed the same had happened as had happened to the eyes of the creature in front of him.

"Fuck this shit!" Emery screamed.

He plunged his sword deep into the dead human's abdomen. It screeched once more, but remained upright. Emery withdrew his sword, and stabbed it again. The creature was unaffected by the sharp sword.

It threw itself at Emery, sending a whiff of its nauseating stench at the blades before it reached him. It clambered on to him, and pushed him to the ground.

"Emery!" Tryden cried out, and stabbed the undead in the head with his sword, but it continued struggling.

Emery pushed the human off of him, and then swung his sword, decapitating it. With its head rolling away, the body remained motionless. No blood came out, but a viscous fluid slowly seeped out.

"By the grace of Athra!" Emery panted, rising to his feet. "What the fuck was that!?"

Tryden pictured the engraving in his mind. "It's one of the ancient ones, I think. We need to get out of here."

"Agreed! Kill them by severing the head, by the way. They don't seem to die from anything else."

"Yeah, I saw," Tryden said. He scanned the area, his eyes now used to the dark. He could see outlines of several more ancient ones. "Let's go, before they come for us!"

Emery and Tryden charged toward the corridor out. They raced past the monsters before the circle was closed. Tryden let his sword go through one as it came to his side. It staggered away, into another one.

The blades rushed through the corridor outside the room, and flew down the stairway. They raced through the hallway beyond, taking the turns and twists that followed, crashing into the walls several times. It was too dark to see anything, even though their eyes had gotten used to it; they were running blind for their lives.

Tryden heard the scuffing behind them. The ancient ones kept up despite their fragile appearance. Then again, maybe they weren't so fragile; one wrestled Emery, a man as strong as three, to the ground and they did not die when they were run through with a sword.

Trying to shut out the dismay of that realization, Tryden emerged onto the bridge leading across the prison complex, with Emery up ahead of him. Faint light washed over them. They could finally see, if only slightly.

Reaching the middle of the narrow bridge, Emery came to a stop. Tryden skidded to a halt, too. "Why are you stopping, Brother Emery?"

"This is a perfect choke point," Emery replied. "We'll hold them here."

Tryden said nothing, but agreed. The bridge was narrow, and with no railings, they could push the ancient ones off it. They would have to deal with the monsters anyway, so here was just as good a place as any.

They turned and faced the darkness from where they had come. They waited for the undead humans. The anticipation was killing them. They had never encountered anything like this before. The one thing worse were faerharti, the humanoid Maenics.

They heard the groan first. Then it came: an ancient one materialized from the blackness. Tryden took in its scrawny, vile appearance, and met its lifeless eyes. Its lips had rotten away, and its foul, yellow teeth were gritted.

The ancient one started for the blades, and the rest of its kind followed. They swarmed onto the bridge, all with a vile, hungering look directed toward the living men. The wall of stench that came from them made Tryden want to vomit; it smelled worse than death.

The ancient ones were undead, like the soulless ones. But there was a difference. Tryden sensed it. The magic that had created the ancient ones was evident; he felt it in the air like a freezing wind. He hadn't felt that with the soulless ones.

The first ancient one leapt toward Emery. It didn't get far. With a smack of the broad side of his sword, it tumbled into the depths beneath the bridge, the squishy thud echoing up several seconds later.

Another one came at Tryden. He stabbed it in the heart. The sticky fluid seeped out, but the beast kept going, sliding farther down the blade. It was unaffected by the weapon; it felt no pain and didn't so much as flinch.

Tryden yanked the sword to the side, ripping the ancient one half open, dried-up organs and viscous fluid flying out. The top of the body fell to the side, still attached to the lower part with a string of dry flesh. The ancient one was alive. It snarled and screeched with its head hanging upside down at its side.

"What the fuck!?" Tryden exclaimed. "How the hell can it be alive!? Even an undead body should need its insides!"

Emery kicked the ancient one off of the bridge. "Who the fuck cares!?"

He sliced an ancient one apart. His sword came back, and chopped another's head clean off. As the second one's head flew in a direction, the body in another, and the lower part of the first one fell off of the bridge, the upper part crawled around on the bridge. It watched him with hungry eyes.

Emery met its eyes. He struck its head with his sword. It did not die. He repeated the strike time and time again; he stabbed the ancient one in the head repeatedly, letting out a war cry at the same time.

With one last strike and a loud crack—the head long ago having become mush—his sword penetrated the very bridge they were on. Cracks spread from where the sword pierced the stone.

Emery looked at Tryden, their eyes connecting. "Fuck."

Big chunks of rock fell off the bridge and crashed into the unknown depths. Emery pulled his sword free, and backed away from the cracks and ancient ones with Tryden.

When a loud crack cut through the sounds of hunger the ancient ones let out, the men spun around and threw themselves to the doorway leading back—safety.

The bridge collapsed; it in its entirety crashed downward. Emery shoved Tryden as hard as he could, and leapt forth. As the latter fell to his knees in safety and the former landed beside him, the bridge and ancient ones tumbled into the darkness.

Merely echoes of the unholy creatures' shrieks remained, and then the thuds of their squishy bodies and the clang of rock against rock. After that, silence settled.

8

Rynus Kalera gawked at the Thalmanian words. "Hirae lajen port til verlen af faer," he mumbled. "Verlen af faer."

His cousin was resting with his back against the wall with the words. He looked feverish; sweat was running down his skin, to which his hair stuck. He even had trouble keeping his eyes open.

"The world of fire," Rynus continued mumbling. "Do you know what that means, Adam?"

"No, what?" Adam slurred, at the brink of incoherence. He was barely lucid.

"I don't want to say it aloud." Rynus swallowed his fear. "I cannot. It is too terrible."

Adam looked at Rynus, trying to keep his stare still. His head wagged from side to side, too heavy for him to hold up straight. "Cousin, I ain't feeling so good."

Rynus stopped looking at the wall, and instead turned to his cousin. He had become worse over the last hour, since the blades left; the sickness was growing.

Rynus could sense no evil magic in Adam. As Tryden had pointed out, this was too quick for an infection. The wound had been dressed with dew moss, so it would be impossible for an infection to settle, unless it was potent and had been introduced directly to the bloodstream.

Rynus's heart dropped when he thought of what caused Adam's wound. A soulless one had torn his flesh with rotten teeth. What germs did those teeth cultivate?

"I didn't come here to steal stuff," Adam stated, still in his state of bare lucidity.

Rynus raised his eyebrows. "You didn't?"

"No, I-I didn't. I came here 'cause ma and pa to-told me to bring you back to 'em. They... told me to come here, Rynus. They told me to."

Rynus's mouth was open, but he could not speak. He just stared at his cousin in silent shock. "Wh-why?"

"They wants their one good son back."

"I'm not their son. You are."

"That ain't how they sees it."

Rynus turned away from Adam, blinking away the tears. All his life, he had overshadowed his cousin. He had led the life that could have been Adam's, should have been his, had Rynus not been there. Adam could have been educated. He could have led a good life.

Instead, he sat on the filthy floor in a fort full of evil, having been bitten by a soulless one. Instead, his parents had sent him to what may be his death to find the good son, the one they liked more.

"I'm sorry, Adam," Rynus said, still with his back turned to his cousin. He dared not look in his eyes; it would be too painful. "I'm so sorry."

"It... It ain't your fault," Adam slurred. "You always taked care of me."

Rynus closed his eyes. "We'll get out of this, Adam. I got you into this, and I'll get you out. I've always felt more like a brother to you than a cousin. I'll take care of you. I'll get you back home. I promise."

No reply.

Rynus sniveled, and opened his eyes. "Adam?"

Still no reply.

He turned around. Adam was still sitting against the wall, but his head sloped to the side and his chest did not appear to be rising and sinking. "Adam? Adam!?"

Rynus dashed to his cousin, falling down to his knees beside him. He grabbed his shoulders, and shook him. "Adam! Wake up, Adam! Damn you!"

Rynus laid Adam on his side, and rolled him to his back. He put an ear to his chest. He heard no beating of his heart. With a growl, he pressed his hands put together and palm down to the chest. Thirty pumps, and he leaned in and blew three deep breaths of air into his cousin's lungs.

"Come on, Adam!" In a moment of hopelessness, he let a cry into the stale air and pounded his fist to Adam's chest, again and again. "Adam! Please don't leave me!"

Adam's eyes came open. Rynus stopped bashing him with his fist. Their eyes met; they gazed into each other; they saw into each other's souls. Only one tear made it down Rynus's cheek.

Adam reached for him. He wrapped his arms around the wizard with an iron hold. With no remorse, Adam sank his teeth into his cousin. Blood and tears rained to the ground, splashing against it in a cry of anguish.

Nothing remained of what used to be.

9

"Precursors damn this place!"

Tryden smiled at Emery's annoyance. "I'm sure we will be there soon."

"Yeah, but don't it feel like the way back is longer? This is fucking dreary."

"I'm sure we'll be back soon."

Emery flexed his muscles. "I wish I had something to kill, just to pass the time."

"I am glad to have the peace. You should also be glad we don't have to fight anything right now. I've got a feeling we'll get our fair share in the not-too-distant future. In fact, we'll probably get more than our fair share."

Emery grunted. "Maybe you're right, brother bookworm." He grinned. "I hope you're right."

Glancing at Emery, Tryden smiled. "You wouldn't mind to stop calling me that, would you?"

Emery's grin widened on his ugly, scarred face, distorting

it even more. "Sorry, brother bookworm, but I would."

"I figured."

They rounded one of the many corners of the dark corridor, and continued onward. It was difficult to find their way in the darkness, now that they didn't have a torch anymore; they could only see a leap or so ahead.

"You know, you are pretty damn strong, Brother Emery," Tryden continued. "It is amazing how you actually destroyed the entire bridge."

"That ain't nothing."

"No, it's something. You're damn strong."

Emery didn't answer. Instead, he looked ahead. "I see the room, I think."

Tryden looked ahead, too. He could see light. Finally, they had reached the end of the long passage; the room they had left Rynus and Adam in was in the distance. Noise echoed to them from the room.

"What is that?" Tryden wondered.

"I don't know," Emery said.

Tryden couldn't quite hear what it was; it was too distant and quiet. What was the sound? It sounded like talking, but no, it was too aggravated, volatile. It was a scream; someone was screaming!

"Someone's screaming!" Tryden shouted, taking off for the room. Nearing it, the sound became more distinguishable. It was definitely a scream, one of pure horror.

Coming into the room, his gaze fell upon the two men in there. They were Rynus and Adam Kalera. What were they doing? Rynus was atop Adam, who hugged him and pressed his face against his shoulder.

No, he was biting him! Adam was biting Rynus; he tasted his flesh and blood. The illness had claimed him in the end. Adam Kalera was a soulless one.

Tryden drew his sword. "Get off of him!"

"Nooo!" Rynus shouted in anguish. "Don't hurt him! Don't hurt my Adam!"

A force wave of magic shot out of the wizard, moved past Adam without hurting him, and knocked Tryden off his feet.

Emery stormed past Tryden, toward the two Kalera cousins, drawing his sword, too.

"Nooo!" Rynus screamed once more.

With a flash of steel, Emery cut through Adam's neck. His warm blood splashed out of his already dead body, and his teeth let go of Rynus's flesh. The body fell onto the ground with a faint thud, only having been a few pacs off of it. The head hit the ground with a louder thud, several leaps away. Massive amounts of blood started pooling around the separate pieces of Adam.

"No!" Rynus shouted. "Why did you do that!?"

"I had to," Emery said calmly. "He was biting you."

Tryden got up on his feet. "I'm so sorry, Rynus. He was a soulless one. He had to be put down."

"That's my cousin you're talking about!"

"He wasn't your cousin anymore, Rynus. His soul was no longer in his body."

Rynus sank down onto the floor. His eyes darted from the dead body of Adam Kalera to the severed head, where they rested for a few moments. He looked into the empty eyes. He broke away, staring at the wall instead; he could not stand seeing the death.

Tryden pulled away Emery. "Let's give him some time."

Emery nodded. "Yeah."

"So where are Master Pleagau and Brother Sizle?"

Emery shrugged. "They'll be here."

"But shouldn't they be here already?"

"As I said, they'll be here."

Tryden looked at Rynus, gave Emery a meaning look, and started pacing back and forth, mumbling the words he had read. "Ock iatil faer vii skael gaht." He felt like they were of importance, but what did they mean?

He looked to the path to the left, the one into which Sizle and Rither had disappeared. Where were they? Tryden and Emery had been gone a long while, and still the others had not returned. Was their wall with Thalmanian words farther away? Or had something happened to them?

"Maybe we should look for them," he suggested.

Emery gave him a look, as if to say the mere thought was treason, an insult to the flawless knight their boss was. As Tryden opened his mouth to argue, he heard footsteps, and soon enough, Rither and Sizle came running for them from the left passage.

"See," Emery said. "Told you they'd be here."

"Get your swords ready!" Rither commanded.

They gawked at him with questioning frowns, which were soon wiped from their faces. Ten ancient ones followed. The pasty skin wrapped too close to their bones sent an impulse of disgust welling up Tryden's throat. He forced it down with a clenched face.

Rynus rose to his feet, breathing heavily and looking from one of the monsters to the next. He drew a deep breath, and let it out in a scream. "Nooo! Fuck you, Kritz!"

They all felt the power he was emitting. His cry of anguish even made the ancient ones halt. A burst of magic exploded from him. The room shook powerfully. Cracks spread from where he stood.

With one final outburst of grief, he sent his magic toward the hallway the ancient ones were coming from. A blue wall of magic crashed into the doorway. A deafening explosion of light and dust threw the guardian blades off their feet.

The passageway collapsed with a thunderous roar, crushing the ancient ones under the weight of all the rocks. Their viscous insides were squeezed out, staining the dirty floor. Their shrieks were barely heard in the ruckus.

Rynus Kalera dropped to the ground once more. His face was now blank; his moment of anger had been swapped out for one of nothingness. Tryden looked from him to the upper bodies of the ancient ones, which still crawled around and were being decapitated by Rither.

"What the hell happened here!?" Sizle wondered.

"That Adam guy had turned into a soulless one when we came back," Emery said. "We had to put him down."

Sizle put a hand over his mouth, glancing at Rynus. "Oh."

Rither joined them, having killed all the ancient ones. "I'm sorry to hear that, but we still have a mission."

"I'm afraid it isn't that simple," Tryden stated. "Adam was bitten by a soulless one, and soon enough turned into one." He lowered his voice to but a whisper. "Adam bit Rynus."

Rither glanced at the wizard. "You think he'll turn?"

"I know I will," Rynus said loudly, still sitting a bit away. "I feel the disease in me. My magic—my soul—is resisting it, but I am afraid it won't be enough. Before long, my soul will depart and all that will be left of me is an evil husk. My only thought will be to spread the disease and bring death to all mortals. Before long, I'll be a soulless one."

10

"We can't let him live! He could turn!"

"We cannot kill a human being, Brother Emery! He's not a soulless one yet!"

"Exactly! Yet! He ain't one yet! As in, he will be soon!"

"Silence, both of you," Rither ordered, looking at the wall with words. "Tryden's right. We can't kill him; he's a human being. Tell me the words instead."

Tryden glared at Emery, before facing Rither. "The words were, 'ock iatil faer vii skael gaht'."

"So the entire phrase is, 'Enaean vii stett maat maenicae, ock iatil faer vii skael gaht'."

"What does it mean?" Sizle wondered.

"It means—"

"That you mortals will die," a voice said, which wasn't just dark, rough, and throaty, but also familiar.

"Od'kel," Rither growled.

Black smoke appeared by the wall with words. It solidified into the Maenic, as tall as any, but looking bigger, with its body fortified by jagged, red armor. Its black skin and sharp features could strike fear in anyone. Its five clawed fingers held the hilt of a broad sword.

The Maenic bowed down. "Mortals, I have been looking for you. Our battle was tragically cut short last we met. Now is the time to finish it."

Emery clenched both fists. "The time for you to die."

"I am afraid death is a concept unknown to us immortals. We cannot learn it, because we cannot die. As for you, mortal, I do not know if your soul is new or not. If it is, I'll have to educate you in death, as you know as little as I."

"There will come a day when demonic immortals such as you will be judged, and your immortality will be taken from you," Rither said, keeping his deadly gaze on Od'kel. "When that day comes, I will be there to watch you fall."

The Maenic smirked as it met Rither's gaze. "And will pigs start to fly, perchance? You don't know how short your time is. One way or another, your time here on Atae will come to an end. The fires of destruction shall sweep across home, as it means in your mortal tongue of Thalman.

"We are hours from our victory here at Gateway Keep. The mortal world will be swallowed by Oblivion, and in the belly of the world of fire, you'll roast. Lord Uhr shall possess your souls. He will annihilate Evengarden and every one of your false gods."

Rither unsheathed his sword. "We'll stop you!"

The Maenic's grim grin grew even wider. "There is nothing you can do. Even if you somehow stop us here, the fight will not yet be over. The last of the dragon hunters will fall, and when he does, the barrier will be broken. Dragons shall rise from their shallow graves and set the world aflame.

"The Machine is nearing completion. With it, the lord who worships us Maenics will break the barrier. He and his kind will awaken the sleeping children of Lord Uhr. They'll let the Maenic lord into the world of mortals, and He shall lead us to victory. Mortals, your days are numbered."

"It is *your* days that are numbered, demon," Rither retorted. "Now prepare to be slain!"

The three other blades also unsheathed their swords. All four stood ready to fight the Maenic. Rither prayed its magic would not be too much. He prayed to all Gods; he prayed to the three Precursors—Athra, Bul, and Sivana—and the ten Divines—Aevala, Althir, Navae, Thundrae, Shae, Falk, Sina, Cuthra, Faemala, and Ridicae. He prayed for the strength to save the world of mortals.

The Maenic hissed, and dashed forward, swinging its big sword at the blades. They backed away from the wide swing, scarcely dodging death. The demon was strong.

It waved its hand to the right, throwing Tryden and Sizle aside using magic. It swung the sword at Emery. He raised his sword to parry, but it was knocked from his hand by the demon's sheer force.

Rither leapt to the demon, piercing its abdomen. It pulled him close, baring its foul teeth. Each stared into the other's eyes with contempt.

Od'kel shoved Rither away several leaps. It pulled out his sword, and threw it to the side. "Curse you, mortal!"

Rynus Kalera stepped forward, placing himself in front of the demon. "We'll finish our duel, now!"

"Oh, the wizard!" Od'kel said, practically skipping up and down. "How fun! I rarely get a fair challenge from one with the gift!"

"You will not have one now either! I'm more than a match to you!"

Dropping its big sword, the Maenic hissed. It charged up an orb of darkness between its hands. With a growl, Rynus charged up one of light between his. Now, they would once and for all determine who the more powerful one was.

They unleashed their magic. The light and dark collided. First, they vanished, and then exploded in a mixture of the two opposite forces of nature. The faerhart and human were thrown away, but were unscathed by the explosion.

They charged up more magic, getting ready to make another attempt on their lives. They were putting their all into this attack; they would either come out on top or die.

Rither charged for Od'kel, and sliced into its neck. Black blood spouted out by the sword's sides. The Maenic gasped for air, but was unable to fill its lungs; the sword blocked its trachea, not to mention having severed blood vessels.

Rither withdrew his sword, and let the Maenic sink to its knees. It looked up at him, still trying to breathe and blood pulsing out to the beat of its unholy heart. Arterial spatter stained Rither in a pattern of tiny droplets reaching across his torso in a pillar.

As Rither turned to Rynus and nodded, it turned to him, too. The wizard was still charging up his magic. He met the demon's cold eyes, and let it go.

Rither could see a look in Od'kel's demonic eyes. What he saw was not fear or anger; it was nothing he had expected. What he saw was the hint of a smug gleam. Od'kel knew as well as he did that even with its death, it would not be over. The war had not yet been won or lost; more battles would be fought before the end.

The magic of light collided with the demon of darkness. It burst open, black blood and flesh spattering many leaps in every direction. A tidal wave of blood and flesh swept across the floor. Only the legs remained, kneeling like when a body was attached. They tipped over, splashing into the recently formed ocean of darkness.

"Holy Gods, that's a lot of blood!" Sizle stuttered.

They all looked about the room, covered in a thick layer of black blood, dotted with flesh and entrails. The Maenic had gone down, but it had stained them with its foulness. Rither spat out a mouthful of the murky, iron-flavored soup, which against his will had been thrown into his mouth. He wiped the blood off his face, and brushed viscera off his shoulders and armor with a clenched frown.

"Yeah," Tryden agreed. "I hope it was painful. I hope that bastard suffered."

"Can we just move on?" Rynus panted, as he staggered to a wall to rest. "I can feel the sickness inside of me growing. Once I turn, I can no longer be of any use to you."

Rither nodded. "I'll speak the words."

He moved to the wall with Thalmanian words. Following Kritz and driving a sword through his black heart was what mattered now. Stopping the plan he had set in motion was even more important. If Od'kel had told them the truth, Siva would be swallowed by Oblivion. How, Rither didn't know. If it indeed were true, it could not be allowed to happen.

Rither continued staring at the wall. He knew they had to

move on, but he was terrified. He knew what waited beyond the stone wall.

Hirae lajen port til verlen af faer. Here lies the doorway to the world of fire. Those were the words inscribed on the wall in front of him. Those were the words that made him shudder, made the hair on the back of his neck rise.

"Boss?" Emery wondered. "Are you okay?"

"Yeah, yeah, I'm fine."

"How about speaking the words, boss? Eanan vi stalt miit maenicae, ock itila whatever."

Rither forced down the big lump in his throat. He had to be strong; he was the leader. Now was the time to show his strength—to lead. "Enaean vii stett maat maenicae, ock iatil faer vii skael gaht!"

His voice echoed through the room. They waited anxiously, the blades fingering the hilts of their swords and Rynus pulling at his wizard's robes, his gaze darting to the remains of his cousin, now covered in black blood.

Nothing happened.

Emery looked from the wall to Rither. "Uhm, boss, what's going on?"

"Don't know," Rither said. "It should've worked. Should it not have worked?"

Rynus shrugged. "It should have worked, unless magic is needed. Let me try." He turned to the wall. "Enaean... Wait, what was it?"

"... vii stett maat maenicae, ock iatil faer vii skael gaht."

"Right. Enaean vii stett maat maenicae, ock iatil faer vii skael gaht." Rynus's words echoed through the room. Once more, nothing happened.

"I don't get it," Sizle said. "Why don't they work? Did the text on the wall not say to use these words?"

Rither translated the words on the wall aloud. "Here lies the doorway to the world of fire. To cease the lockdown, say the words of unholy magic to the right and left."

"Exactly. So it did say to do that. Why won't it work?"

Tryden pulled a hand through the hair on the back of his head. "Maybe—"

"What are you thinking?" Rither asked.

"We took their literal meaning as a direction, and traveled to the right and left to find new words."

"What of it?"

"What if it's not only a literal direction, but a riddle? Perhaps we're supposed to say the sentence backward."

Rither put a wide grin on his face. "This is why I like having you on the team, Gelan. You're smart."

"Thank you, Master Pleagau."

"It is definitely worth a try. Okay, here goes," Rither said, facing the wall again. He cleared his throat. "Thag leaks iiv reaf litai kco, eacineam taam ttets iiv naeane."

The words echoed throughout the room, and then silence settled. Rither felt his heart pound inside of his chest and a tingling sensation in his stomach.

Once more, nothing happened.

"Damn it! How is this gate ope—"

With a loud crack, the wall parted in two. A cloud of dust filled the room as the scraping of rock against rock filled the men's ears. When the cloud of dust settled and the scraping stopped, Rither saw stairs beyond the wall, where an opening now existed.

"Holy... You were right, Brother Tryden."

This time it was Tryden's turn to smile at Rither. "Have I ever been wrong, Master Pleagau?"

"I guess you haven't."

The five men moved to the opening with the stairs down. Unlike the rest of the fort, it was bright. At the bottom of the stairway, a disc of fire was suspended a bit over the ground. Its outlines burned with bright flames, which turned flatter and darker toward its middle, having a dot of pure darkness at its very center.

Seeing into what he could only call a portal of fire, Rither was reminded of the baldran's fiery eyes. Looking into them had felt like it felt beholding the portal. He knew what waited for them beyond, and they had no choice but to go there; too much was at stake.

"You never did say what the words mean," Sizle said, unable to drag his eyes off of the fiery gate.

"That's right," Tryden concurred. "You didn't."

Emery nodded along. "So what do they mean, boss?"

Rither met each of their eyes, and turned his gaze back to the portal of darkness and flames. "You want to know what 'Enaean vii stett maat maenicae, ock iatil faer vii skael gaht' means?"

"Yes," all of them answered eagerly. Even Rynus looked to Rither, with wild curiosity in his eyes, despite the grief that dampened their luster.

Rither kept his stare on the portal of fire, gazing deep into its volatile dance. The first words echoed through his mind once again—the world of fire. "United we stand against the unholy, and into the fire we shall go."

INTO THE FIRE

1

Together, they stepped into the fire. Flames enveloped them; they became one with fire. As if he were falling, Rither felt a tingle in his stomach. He and the others flew through a fiery tunnel, forever but for a moment. They floated through time and space.

They touched ground, and did so hard. Their legs buckled, and they fell to the ground. Rither shut his eyes to stop the spinning, and swallowed the nausea welling up from his stomach. He opened up his eyes, and looked around.

They were in a large room, made of the same architecture as Fort Lockdown. It had three intact walls, and was high to the ceiling. The forth wall, the one straight ahead, had collapsed, with part of the ceiling. Debris littered the floor, and cracks stretched along the walls.

What he saw through the opening made his heart skip a beat; it made all his fears about what the portal led to come true. Black clouds were in the hell-red sky. Swarms of black birds flew through it.

"Where the hell are we!?" Sizle wondered.

Rither rose to his feet, turning only lopsidedly to the other men. "You just answered your own question."

"What? How so?"

"We're in hell—Oblivion."

Sizle's eyes turned wide. "What!? Are you serious!?"

Rither just nodded, and turned to the hole in the wall. In the distance, he could see a tower. A red aura surrounded its top, and a beam reached all the way from it to the portal of fire behind them. Even farther away, a wall of red towered up high into the sky.

"What do you suppose the beam does?" Tryden wondered. "And that weird wall?"

Rynus shrugged. "Maybe it's widening the portal, so it will be big enough for Oblivion itself to make it through. I do not know about the wall."

"That is incorrect," a voice said. "You're close to the truth, though."

They looked around to see who had spoken. Angus Kritz descended through the air, landing on the ground without a sound. His monstrous face was locked in a tight smile, and his black and white eyes studied the five men before him.

"I see you're a man short," he said. "How terribly sad."

Rither drew his sword. He noted how Rynus clenched his hands into fists, but chose not to dignify the remark with a response himself. Instead, he inquired, "Do you know what it does, perchance?"

Kritz met Rither's eyes with his inhuman ones. "What you see behind you is a portal between Oblivion and Siva. Only because the barrier between the two worlds is weak here is it possible for this link to even exist."

Kritz gestured around the room with his arms held wide apart, and then nodded to the outside. "This entire area is a weakness in the barrier, but it's not yet big enough for most Maenics to make it through. The wall of light embodies this; it is a physical manifestation of the barrier. The area looks big, but spiritually, the hole is not yet wide enough."

"And the beam," Rither said, "it holds the portal open?"

Kritz smiled. "Precisely. The aura about the tower is what weakens the barrier. Should the crystal powering the beam be shattered, the portal will destabilize and close."

"How long has this been going on?"

"You ask the question as if to say how long I've been at it. It isn't my plan. Fort Lockdown was built during the reign of dragons. Of course, it was called Gateway Keep back then. The dragons had it built because the barrier is weak here. It was their intention to bring Oblivion into Siva.

"Before this could happen, your false gods bestowed upon you a gift; mortals were given the gift of magic. Aevira were given the gift by Aevala. She gave the gift to all Her children, which is why all of them have magic weaker than that of a human. Althir bestowed His gift upon mankind, but did not give it to everyone. This is why gifted ones are rare but very powerful.

"I am not a gifted one myself. I wasn't blessed with magic from birth. I prayed to Lord Uhr, and He gave me the gift, so I could finish what His sons and daughters started.

"One more kind of gifted ones, also only humans, came to be, but how is not entirely known, at least not to me. These were dragon hunters. They turned the tide of the war; only they were strong enough to take on dragons.

"When the war was over, the olden order of the Guardian Blades took Gateway Keep, renamed it Fort Lockdown, and sealed off the weak spot. The remaining power and rumors created by the secrecy of the Guardian Blades led many to try and take it. Much blood was spilled over the fort. In the end, no one got it. It was erased from time itself.

"The people who came to the fort later did not even know what it was; they did not know of its power. Lucky for them, the bone guards created by Drahc Uhr—the ancient ones—slumbered. Only when disturbed would they wake up to kill; until I released them from their slumber, that is."

Rither clenched his jaw, and tightened the grip of the hilt of his sword. "Now you've opened the gates. You want to let loose the hordes of Oblivion. Why?"

Kritz's face turned vile. He spat on the ground before him. "Drahc Uhr is the true god! The Divines and Precursors are false!" He calmed himself with a deep breath. "When I was a young man, I lived in the Kayan Isles, under the rule of Lord Culous Alamain. He was murdered, and a tyrant seized the throne."

"Adrian Alamain," Rynus growled.

"Under his rule, the Kayan Isles turned to hell—murders, rapes, tortures... injustice. It opened my eyes to the world. I realized that under the rule of the wrong gods, chaos would ensue. Only with the firm reign of Drahc Uhr will chaos become stability."

"You can't blame the sins of mortals on the Gods!" Rither shouted. He closed his eyes. "Help us stop this, Angus, before it is too late. Help us close the portal again. Do at least one honorable thing in your life."

"It's too late. The weak spot cannot be resealed from Siva; it is too weak. Soon, it will be big enough for Lesser Maenics to make it through. Not long thereafter, Oblivion shall swallow Siva whole, like a shark that swallows a strada fish."

"I refuse to believe that. It can't be too late."

"It is. Even if the gateway is closed, the hole in the barrier is much too wide and frail. Sooner or later, the Maenics will break through. We have won."

"We? You mean you and the Maenics?" Tryden asked. He laughed. "You say that like you are one of them. Do you not realize they are only using you? You're just a pawn to them. You're nothing but another filthy mortal."

"Yeah," Emery agreed. "The three Maenics admitted they were in Siva to babysit you, and that, if you fail, which you will, there's another plan in motion, too."

"And we'll foil not only this plan, but also that other one," Sizle joined in, and then added, "Whatever it may be."

"I know about it," Kritz said, an unwavering smile on his lips. "There is a prophecy. A battle is coming, and it'll start, and perhaps even end, with two people. That is, if the war is not won here, today, in the realm of Oblivion."

"With whom will the next battle start?" Tryden asked.

"You think I'll tell you?"

"I suppose not."

"Tell you what, I have a third and final challenge for you," Kritz said, his smirk growing wider. "If you defeat me in fair combat, five against one," his eyes wandered from one of the men to the next, "I will tell you the names. Hell, I'll even tell you what you can do."

"Deal," Rither growled.

Emery's countenance flinched in anger and hatred. "Then you die, Kritz."

The old wizard smiled at Emery, and let his eyes fall upon the others, too. Between his vile smile, inhuman eyes, and magic, he was a heart-chilling man. His soul was corrupted; it had grown bitter. Angus Kritz was evil to his core.

With a snarl, he threw his arms forward, sending a burst of embers at the five men. They shielded their faces from the leaves of fire. When they looked again, he was gone.

Tryden, Emery, and Sizle drew their swords, too, and all of them stood ready. Rynus readied fire magic in his hands; they lit like when he had been their torch. Then they waited for Kritz to make his move.

Rither felt his heart pound hard in his chest. Every cell in his being was vibrating in fear and excitement. He had long sought to kill Kritz. Now that he waited for what may be his death, he yearned to be away from there. He wanted to be in the safety of Siva; he wanted to be in her soft embrace, feel her firm ground underneath his feet, and fill his lungs with her fresh air.

He had to stay and fight, though. Angus Kritz had to die; it was that simple. They had to kill him, and stop the weak spot in the barrier from widening further. If they could not, all would be lost.

An orb of blue magic thundered through the air, like electricity. It crashed into the floor with an explosion, narrowly missing its targets. Splinters of rock and dust were cast into the air, forcing the men to stagger away.

Another magical orb was shot from seemingly nowhere in the air above. Rither could not see from where it had come, just that it was coming for them. He couldn't see Kritz.

Rynus Kalera stepped forward, and put up his hands. A transparent, blue force field came to be, which Kritz's magic collided with. A blue thunderstorm exploded through the air when they met, but quickly died off, leaving the hot and dry air electric.

Rynus let the force field die away, and then sent a fireball into the air, seemingly toward nothingness. The fire collided with something, and a scream followed. Angus Kritz became visible, and crashed to the ground. Flames enveloped him, but he didn't seem to take notice. He rose to his feet. With a spasm, he shrugged off the fire.

The two wizards glared at each other. The older one lit his hands on fire, just like the younger one's already were. They moved their fingers like waves across their hands in anticipation of who would make the first move.

In the blink of an eye, both raised their arms and thrust them forward. Continuous flames burst out of their hands. The fire collided in between them, and exploded in a volatile blaze of chaos.

A sphere of concentrated fire took shape. Flickers of fire erupted from the hot star, quickly dying off in the arid air. Fire dripped to the floor, burning holes in the rock there. It was the most powerful magic Rither had ever seen. Oblivion was fuel to the fire.

They couldn't wait, in case Kritz would win the duel. Then they would stand no chance, not against that power. Rither signaled the other guardian blades to move in toward Kritz, and they approached him with their swords ready.

Rither swung his at the seemingly defenseless wizard, but the gifted one waved one arm toward him, keeping the other toward Rynus and the fireball. Rither felt something hit his chest, and then he was on the floor several leaps away. He did not know how he got there. His body ached, pain radiating from his chest, and he struggled to breathe.

Sizle and Tryden closed in for the kill. Kritz moved both of his arms to the fire, and slashed them aside. The fire parted to the sides; the sphere of fire split apart. The blades had to duck under the flames.

The fire magic went wild; strings of flames danced around in the hazy air as if they had a life of their own. Rynus desperately tried to gain control of it.

With the threat of being burned alive gone, Kritz sent one pulse wave to Sizle and one to Tryden, throwing them away through the air. He turned his full attention on the younger wizard again.

Kritz had just enough time to see the blue orb being flung to him. He caught it, and sent it back. Rynus was hit by his own spell, which exploded on impact. He was thrown to the ground, alive only because he managed to shield himself.

Kritz set his hands aflame, and let fire explode from them. Flames melted the air between him and Rynus. The younger wizard would be burned to death; flames would take his life before the sickness afflicting him could. It would be over in mere moments.

"Over here, you bastard!"

Kritz saw Emery by his side, and felt a sword go through his guts. His blood stained the floor, and he tasted it in his mouth. He collapsed to the floor, unable to control his body; it went limp. His fire became a puff of fleeting smoke.

Rither, Tryden, Sizle, and Rynus rose up to their feet, and joined Emery by Kritz. The old wizard tried to do the same, falling over numerous times. In the end, he managed to balance himself.

"We've beaten you," Rither stated. "Tell us about the other plan. Tell us with whom it'll start and what we can do."

Kritz forced a smile to his lips. "This is not over yet. You haven't beaten me until I am dead."

A blinding light filled Rither's eyes; he couldn't see. When the light faded, he saw only his blades and Rynus. They all blinked at each other. Angus Kritz was gone.

"What the fuck!" Emery exclaimed. "Where'd he go!?"

They looked around in search of a sign of him. They saw one: a trail of blood led from where Angus Kritz had been to the portal of fire.

"He's gone back to Siva," Tryden said. "The coward fled."

Emery clenched his jaw and tightened the grip around his sword. "We gotta go after him! That bastard has to die!"

Rither shook his head. "We have more pressing matters."

"Like what!?"

"Like the portal between Oblivion and Siva, the beam that keeps it open, and the magic aura that weakens the barrier; they are more of a problem than Kritz."

"We must do away with what is causing the beam and the aura," Tryden said. "We can't let the weakness grow, or—as Kritz and the Maenics said—Siva will be swallowed whole by Oblivion."

Rither looked to the tower in the distance. They had to go

through the wastes of Oblivion to get to it; they had to walk through fire.

"Everyone is counting on us. We can't let them down," he said. "Even if we die and our souls are lost here forever, we cannot let this go on. The hordes of Oblivion will never walk Atae. We are the guardians that stand against them; we are the Guardian Blades of Siva."

2

Rither was climbing up on a scorching, big rock. A hundred leaps behind him, at the bottom of the hill, lay the ruins of Gateway Keep, the portal of fire clearly visible. They had left it to venture into Oblivion.

It was not truly Oblivion; it was a middle ground between Oblivion and Siva. A few hundred leaps away in every direction, a wall of red light marked the end of the scenery they were treading through.

It was difficult for Rither to imagine how Lesser Maenics, and even Greater Maenics, couldn't make it into this area; it was so big. As a mortal, he had only a grasp of the physical. The weakness in the barrier was not of physical nature. The area closed off by the red wall was a physical representation of the weakness, not of how big it was.

Reaching the top of the big rock, an expanse of wasteland opened up before him. A sandy road led through the landscape with twists and turns, all the way to the tower in the distance. It was enclosed by jagged cliffs and rocks the first half, and then a field of what looked like red grass. The tower they had to reach was on the far side of the field.

Followed by the others, Rither slid down the rock, stumbling onto the road below. The heat from the ground easily made it through the soles of his boots. The air that filled his lungs burned. To keep his eyes from drying, he had to blink constantly.

They silently made their way along the road. They dared not speak. They barely dared to draw breath. Encountering

Maenics was one thing, but treading through Oblivion was another thing altogether. As far as Rither knew, no one had ever done so, except sinners sent there for punishment.

The blades had their swords ready. Rynus had his magic. If anything should come for them, they would defend themselves. Every single one was expendable, but they could not die before their mission was finished.

Rither looked up at the red sky. He let his eyes follow one of the many black clouds, before a flock of birds caught his attention. He didn't know what they were, so he let his gaze follow them. They showed no signs of aggression, but maybe they weren't meant for combat.

Something else caught his eyes. The birds were not alone in the hellish skies. But he couldn't make out what it was; it was merely a dot. Was it another swarm of birds far away or something entirely different?

Something crashed into Rither. He fell to the ground with the thing atop him. Saliva dripped onto him. Looking up, he saw a beast.

It was a hound with a smoky, black aura around it. Black fur covered its four legs and lower body, seamlessly turning into dark scales atop its head and back, reaching to its tail, which was bifurcated, each tip ending in a metal spike.

The hound growled, showing the many sharp teeth in its long snout. It glared with its piercing, red-glowing eyes.

Rither shoved the beast off of himself, and stumbled away from it. The hound howled, and took off for the cover of the cliffs. Its howl was answered; it was not alone.

"A devlion," Tryden informed the others.

"What's that?" Sizle wondered.

"It is what you just saw—a Beast Maenic that looks like a hound, with half its body covered in scales."

"It fled," Emery said. "Ain't nothing but a coward."

Tryden shook his head. "They hunt in packs and are very smart. It tested our strength. They'll come for us now, and will do so with speed, force, and precision."

Sizle tried to push down the lump stuck in his throat. "So we're screwed?"

"We're not screwed, Brother Sizle," Rither said. "We're going to make it."

Rynus scanned the area, seeing nothing but the cliffs and rocks. "There are at least a dozen of them out there."

"How do you know?"

"I can sense them, their magic. They are Maenics after all, divine beings, so they are magic by their very nature."

Rither looked around, too, but he was not a gifted one; he couldn't tell if there were any Maenics beyond the rocks. He would have to take Rynus's word for it. "Let's get going."

He led the others onward. The cliffs surrounding the path had dozens of wide cracks. Devlions could come out of any of them. They could very well come from all, if there were as many as Rynus had said.

A howl made Rither shudder, chilling him to his core. The devlions were ready for the hunt. They needed to feed. They needed to sink their teeth into warm flesh to taste the blood seeping out.

"Fuck it," Rither said, "run!"

With swords drawn and magic ready, the men took off for the tower. If they broke free from the cliffy area, the devlions would not be able to attack them with surprise; they needed to reach the field of grass beyond the cliffs.

A devlion came from in between two rocks. Rither noticed the red-glowing eyes first, then the smoky aura, and finally the sharp teeth gleaming with a coat of saliva. Crashing into Tryden, it pushed him face first into a rock and went for his neck with its snout full of sharp teeth.

Emery took hold of the devlion, and threw it away to the side. He helped the bloodied Tryden to his feet. Blood flooded out of his cracked nose.

The devlion rose to its paws, and growled. It got ready to attack yet again. It had the undivided attention of all five of its prey.

And then came the second attack. Another devlion lunged off of a cliff above them, flying toward Sizle with deadly precision. It landed on top of him, pushing him down.

Rynus threw a fireball at the first devlion. The fire hit the hound, flames enveloping it. After a couple moments, with a shrug of its massive body, the hound made the fire die off. It was unscathed by the flames.

Emery thrust his sword into the heart of the hound atop Sizle. The sword met its flesh and black blood. The creature let out a panicked and painful whine, before it fell silent.

The first devlion took off for the safety of the surrounding cliffs, but before reaching them, Rither chopped off its head. The head rolled away, leaving behind a trail of black blood, and the body fell to the ground with a thud, a pool of blood building up around the open neck.

"Fire is no good," Rynus said, glancing at the decapitated devlion, as if it reminded him of something. "They could also be resistant to others types of magic, but I hope not."

Emery snorted, as if wanting the stench of magic, or perhaps devlion, out of his nostrils. "Steel kills 'em."

Sizle crawled to his feet, wiping off the blood on his face. "They can easily kill us, too."

"So far, the body count is two to nothing. I'd say we ain't got nothing to worry 'bout. Right, boss?"

Rither did not reply. He was neither as sure nor confident as Emery, even though he put up a tough exterior to seem as such. They had faced only two devlions. At least ten were out there, and magic was ineffective.

Another thought came to his mind. They were in Oblivion, so what happened to the souls of the killed Maenics? When a Maenic soul-summoned into Siva was slain, its soul would travel to Una, the home to departed souls and only link between the three planes of existence—Siva, Evengarden, and Oblivion. Then it would be sent back to the world of fire.

They were now already in Oblivion. Would the beasts just come back as they were slain? Did their souls have to recuperate before they could build new physical shells?

Rither shook the thought out of his head. It would do no good to worry about something of which he had no control. Should he meet his demise in Oblivion, it would be fine; as long as they stopped the widening of the barrier's weakness, it would be fine.

"We have no time to waste," he said, yet again setting his sight upon the tower. "We must get to that power crystal."

Shadows flew past them. He could see them only with his peripheral vision. They were so quick they were gone before he could turn his head. The remaining devlions, the infernal hounds of Oblivion, were hunting them.

The men took off for the tower. Rither felt his heart pound in his chest. He heard it pulsate in his ears. The faint taste of blood was in his mouth.

A devlion leapt for them from a cliff. With only the grace of the Gods, Rither dodged its teeth, and it smashed snout first into a rock instead. It rose to its paws, shrugged off the pain, and disappeared into a space between the rocks.

Another hound lunged at them. Rynus sent an orb of blue magic at it. They crashed into each other, the magic exploding in a blinding light. Most of the devlion was thrown away, smoke oozing from the dismembered carcass.

The men gave little attention to the sickening, dead soul; they raced past it, fleeing from its brethren still on the hunt. They took slight turns to the left and right, continuing along the twisting and turning path laid out before them. A couple dozen leaps ahead, Rither saw the field of red grass.

A devlion jumped out, placing itself between them and the field. Another blocked off the way back. Rither wrapped his hand tighter around his sword's hilt. They had nowhere to run; blood had to be shed, human or Maenic, red or black.

"This should not be too difficult," Emery said. "I'll take the one behind us, and you guys the one in front. It should be a fair fight, me against one and all of you against the other."

"It's too easy," Tryden mumbled.

"Duck!" Rither screamed.

As the devlions ran into cracks, a couple more came from the sides. Their red-glowing eyes were fixed on their prey.

Tryden ducked to avoid the sharp teeth of one of the demonic hounds. When it was above him, he rose up, bashing his back into its stomach and sending it flying.

The other one came toward Emery. He did not bother with ducking. The Beast Maenic met his sword before it had the chance to bite. The animal swallowed the sharp steel. Black blood flooded out of its snout, and more spattered out of its back, where the sword came out.

Tryden finished off the one he had tackled, stabbing it in its heart and twisting his sword to make sure it wouldn't get back up. "I told you it was too easy. Devlions are smart, and use teamwork to tackle prey."

Emery leaned in toward Tryden with a bloody smile on his face. "They're dead."

Sizle backed into Emery, but before the large man could torture him about it, his eyes fell on the same thing Sizle's already had. Devlions were all around them. A dozen—more than Rynus had predicted—were there. They had cut off the men in all directions; there was nowhere to run.

Rither spun around, looking from one demon to the next. He didn't know how they would get out of it. He didn't know how they would be able to kill that many.

The devlions growled, baring their sharp teeth and staring down their prey with hungry, demonic eyes. Saliva dripped onto the ground, but the glistening coat on their teeth never lessened. The hounds bent their front legs to be closer down to the ground, getting ready for the kill.

Rither saw his fear and that of the others mirrored in the beasts' eyes; everyone but Emery was visibly scared. Rither couldn't help putting a smile on his lips; he was still scared, but Emery's lack of expression made him grin.

A shriek pounded at their ears. It caught the attention of all the hounds; they gazed up at the sky and sniffed the air. With a whine, they took off, disappearing as quickly as they had come, if not quicker.

Emery looked to the last hound as it disappeared behind a rock, and turned to the others. "What the hell?"

Tryden shook his head, still with the horrified look on his face; he couldn't remove it. "I don't know."

Rither studied the sky. He did not see anything there, but they had all heard the shriek. What was it the devlions were afraid of? What could be more dangerous than a whole pack of hellish hounds?

3

The expanse of red grass and cliffs was behind them. They had reached the tower with the mystic aura, from which the beam came that held open the portal back to Siva.

The devlions had not bothered them after the shriek had scared them away. Rither hadn't even seen them. They had really been scared by the shriek. He could only assume that it had been a much deadlier Maenic.

Rither shut out his fear of Maenics to focus on the tower. The black tower was round in shape and the broadest at its bottom, thinning out higher up, but thickening a little at its top. Spikes—mostly colored black with red tips—reached up around it in intervals.

Rither looked back. Now on a hill with red grass, he could see the ruined fort that held the portal leading back to Siva. Stretching from all the way behind it, around the area and the tower, and back behind the fort, the red barrier reached skyward.

He was amazed how they were in Oblivion—as close to it as possible, at least—and the red wall was the barrier.

He let his eyes wander along the skyline. Following a flock of birds, he saw it; the dot he had seen flew through the hot air. It was closer now, bigger. But he still couldn't make out what it was.

Rither turned to the tower's open gateway. He stepped inside, and was met by overwhelming feelings of anxiety and fear. Stairs led up along the walls, supported by no pillars. They led dizzyingly high up to the tower's top. Each triangle-shaped step was the widest by the wall and had a space of nothingness before the next one.

Rither took a careful step onto the stairway, and stopped to look back at the others. "We are near the end, gentlemen. We need only be brave a few more moments."

"We also need to make it back," Sizle said. "Right?"

Rither met Rynus's eyes. Both knew what might happen

once they would destroy the power crystal.

Emery gave Sizle a rough pat on the back. "Of course we'll make it back, runt."

Rither stepped off the stairway, back to the others. He put a hand on Sizle's shoulder. "We'll make it back, Anthony."

Sizle put a gentle smile on his face. "Oh, I never doubted that, Master Pleagau."

Tryden looked from Rynus to Rither, and then looked to Sizle with a warm smile. "Yeah, but first we've got to shatter the crystal at the tower's top."

Sizle nodded, looking to the stairs. With a grotesque smile from Emery, which made him appear more frightened than strengthened, Sizle started up the staircase. Emery followed him, and then also Rynus and Rither, but before they could make it too far, Tryden cleared his throat softly. The master blade and wizard stopped and looked back, while the other guardian blades continued upward.

"What is it, Brother Tryden?" Rither wondered.

Tryden looked to Emery and Sizle. They were still heading upward, unknowing the others weren't with them. "Master, I want the truth. I saw the look on your faces. Why you didn't tell Sizle, I can understand, but you can tell me."

Rither looked to Rynus yet again, and then met Tryden's eyes. He smiled a sad smile. "You're no fool, Gelan."

"No, I'm not."

Rither slowly filled his lungs with arid air, and let all of it out in a heavy sigh. "It's as you fear, Gelan. Once we shatter the crystal, there is a chance the portal will destabilize and close before we can make it back out."

"So, we may be stuck here forever?"

"If that is a problem for you, and you want to go back, I'd suggest you do so now," Rynus cut in. "Oblivion is no place for cowards; nor is the Order of the Guardian Blades."

Tryden gave him a look of pure contempt. "I just needed to know." He pushed past the wizard, shoving him with his shoulder, and made his way up the stairs.

With his mouth open, Rynus looked to Rither. "I thought blades were supposed to be obedient."

"Obedience is the shackles that hold idiots in place. Enslaved idiots do not win wars; soldiers do," Rither stated. He looked to Tryden, who had caught up to the others. "Gelan Tryden Tris is no idiot; nor is he a coward."

With those words, the blade master headed up, jogging to catch up to his disobedient knights. He was proud of them; every one of them showed immense strength.

Gelan Tryden Tris was as brave as he was intelligent. He was of royal blood, but had a level head. He saw himself as an equal to all people and peoples. His sense of loyalty and individuality made him a very useful ally.

Emery Manden was probably the bravest of them all, and definitely the strongest. He was a machine with a human's heart pumping blood through him; he was as human as he appeared inhuman. Rither had known him the longest, and would place his life in his hands, above all else.

Anthony Sizle was the one most easily frightened, but still he would never abandon his blade brothers. While he might have appeared to be the weakest card in the card house—an unstable foundation—he was as strong as any. Between his fear and loyalty, he was one of the bravest people Rither had had the pleasure to know. However, he was unproven, and needed to harden to keep his place as a guardian blade.

Rynus caught up to Rither, and they slowed their pace to walk a couple leaps after the others. "You know, Rither, you are wise."

Rither raised his eyebrows. "I am?"

"I'm sorry. I shouldn't have implied that Tryden is a coward. Of course he isn't."

"Don't worry about it. We're all a little scared."

Rynus stroked his long, blond hair behind an ear. "I suppose you're right. We are in Oblivion."

Rither caressed his beard and scanned Rynus. *The wizard has become pale quickly. How could a distressed heart hope to battle an infection?* "I am sorry about your cousin. I take full responsibility for his passing."

"Don't say that. It was my fault."

"He was my responsibility, as are you. The only reason he

was bitten was because he saved me."

Rynus sighed. "It isn't your fault. He was here because of me. You saved us both; had you not freed us from that cell, Kritz would've sacrificed us to soul-summon more Maenics. That's the only perceivable motive why he didn't execute us. I love... loved Adam, but his death for your life—" The next word got stuck in his throat. "It was for the best. He was an illiterate farmer. You are a master of the Guardian Blades of Siva."

Rither shook his head. "I am not worth more than anyone else. My job is to safeguard our world and its people from... this. That makes me expendable."

The end of the stairs came into view. A hole in the tower's ceiling led to the roof. They headed there, and took the final steps to the top of the tower.

The wide level lay bare underneath the red sky with black clouds. Spikes led around the edge of the tower, forming a railing. At the roof's center, half a dozen pillars around a red crystal held up a spiky roof.

The crystal glowed ominously red, and an aura surround-ed it. A beam was routed from the crystal to a smaller one, attached to the railing, after which it ran all the way to the portal, far away.

"We are finally here," Rither stated, staring at the crystal. "We'll soon end it."

A shriek pounded against his ears. Rither gazed up at the sky, seeing the black dot again, still far away. He hoped that the creature wouldn't find them, whatever it was. The sound of it made his blood turn to ice, even in the blazing warmth of Oblivion.

He looked at Rynus Kalera, Anthony Sizle, Gelan Tryden, and Emery Manden. He trusted the latter three with his life, and had a good feeling about the wizard. All five would end it together. Shutting the portal, the lockdown established by the guardian blades of old would hopefully take effect.

Rither prayed their sacrifice would be the end; he prayed no one would open the gateway again. But Kritz was alive, like a lot of other Maenic worshippers. No amount of wishful thinking would make them vanish; no amount of praying to the Gods would mean victory for the side of good.

Only persistence, bravery, and sacrifice would.

4

Rither's sword cut through the air, but stopped with a clang when it hit the big, red-glowing crystal. Not even a scratch was visible on its surface. They were all gathered under the roofed area, by the crystal. Even with four swords, it would not be demolished. They had been at it for minutes, without making a single mark on it.

"Back off," Rynus said. "Maybe my magic can destroy it."

They backed off, out between the pillars holding the small roof. Rynus raised his hands, and charged up an orb of blue light. He made it as powerful as he possibly could. He threw it to the crystal. When they collided, the orb bounced back. He threw himself aside to avoid his own magic.

"Steel won't work. Magic won't work," Sizle said. "Nothing works!"

"Something has to work," Rither said. "It has to."

The loud shriek pounded at his ears, once more. He spun around, searching for the source of the sound. Then he saw it, the black dot from before. It was closer now, suspended in the air a couple dozen leaps away.

Its body was humanoid, but longer and, in comparison to its length, thinner. It had two long arms and legs, all ending in long, thin fingers and toes, consisting in their entirety of sharp claws. Its complexion was black, but Rither could not tell if it was smooth or scaly. The Maenic must have been at least five leaps from its feet to its head.

A pair of wings attached to its back beat the air around it to keep it from falling. They were the broadest at their tops, thinning out in the shape of a triangle with rounded sides to their bases, where they were broader than just prior.

A thin tail—even longer than its legs—reached down from its lower back, and ended with two sharp and deadly spikes.

A slash from that tail could easily bring death.

Its neck was long, ending with a reptilian head that had a long snout with sharp teeth. It had a couple blood-red eyes, gleaming in the crystal's aura, but not glowing like the eyes of some Maenics.

All in all, the creature looked vile. It was the biggest and most fearsome Maenic the men had ever faced.

"A desdrak," Rynus stuttered. "The dark angel of death, a child of Drahc Uhr, like the dragons."

Rither stared into the Maenic's blood-red eyes, swallowing the lump in his throat. "If a Maenic of this much power can make it through, time is short. We should be glad it is not a dragon."

"I don't think it matters if it's a dragon or not," Sizle stuttered. "Not when we're dead."

The desdrak let out a loud shriek, which bored its way into their heads. The five men put their hands over their ears trying to shield themselves, but it didn't work; instead, they staggered about in blind confusion.

The shrieking ceased, and they fell down. Everything was spinning for Rither; he could not focus. He saw three of the Maenic. For each one, a red dot appeared by its head.

Rither forced his eyes shut, and opened them again. The spinning ceased, but the nausea it had given him remained. He could see the desdrak. A red dot slowly grew stronger in its open mouth.

"Run!" Rither shouted, dragging Sizle to his feet.

They ran as quickly as they could for the six pillars holding up the small roof. They threw themselves into the small, enclosed area, hiding behind the pillars.

The Maenic closed its mouth when the red dot was at its strongest, and drew back its head. Then it forced it forward and opened its mouth. Blazing flames erupted out of it, enveloping the roofed area with constant flames.

When the desdrak stopped breathing its fire, the area was scorched. No movement met its eyes. Rither looked out from behind his cover, seeing the large Maenic. He looked to the others. They were all okay.

"We need to kill the desdrak," he said. "We can't stay here forever. We need to shatter the crystal."

"Agreed," Rynus said. "But I don't see how you could be of any help in this battle; the desdrak flies."

Rither looked out from behind the cover yet again. He met the desdrak's blood-red eyes; it met his blue ones. It opened its mouth to show a red dot. In search of an angle to kill its prey, it started flying around the tower.

"Move!" Rither shouted. "Don't let it find an angle!"

They moved from behind one pillar to the next, keeping it between themselves and the circling predator. It was a game of cat and mouse, or rather Maenic and human or immortal and mortal.

Abruptly, the desdrak switched direction in which it flew. The men stumbled to a stop, also trying to switch direction, before it was too late. The Maenic let loose its fire. Its flames licked the stone ground, the pillars, and the crystal. The fire burned everything it touched to a smoky crisp.

The fire died off. All that remained was smoldering blackness. The desdrak flew closer, trying to find the carcasses of its prey. But it couldn't see them; all it saw were the burned ground and red-glowing crystal.

A crack spread from the center of the crystal. More cracks appeared all over it. The light inside it glowed brighter. The desdrak shrieked into the hazy air, and flew away from the tower and the destruction.

Tryden rose to his feet, having hidden behind the crystal. "It's flying away. Why?"

"I do not know," Rither said, also rising to his feet. "But it did our job for us."

One final crack spread across the surface of the crystal, and when it stopped, everything seemed to stop. Strong, red light broke free from every crack.

"Do you remember what happened when we destroyed the power crystals keeping up the barrier?" Tryden asked. "You know, Kritz's first challenge."

"Yeah," Sizle said. "They... exploded!"

The five men looked at each other and then at the crystal.

They took off for the stairs. Behind them, the light from the cracks grew stronger and then faded away. The crystal was sucked into itself; merely a tiny dot of bright light was left— a singularity of magic.

The men flew down the stairway. They took many steps at once, risking taking a wrong step and falling to their deaths. They had to; it was their only chance. The desdrak had fled because it knew of the power the crystal had.

The singularity exploded. Light drenched the surrounds. Everything touched was destroyed; it was broken into particles, vanishing into inexistence.

The men launched themselves out of the tower. The blast knocked them off their feet. They hit the grassy ground several leaps away, beat up but alive. Behind them, the tower was falling to pieces, its magic aura vanishing.

5

Rither drew in one deep breath after the other to sustain his running pace. His feet hit the ground hard, one before the other. Each time his foot set down to the ground, he heard the rough thud. He and the others dashed across the field of red grass.

The calm sky dotted here and there with black clouds had come to life with a thunderstorm, spiraling around the sky. It was a black mess, one massive cloud spinning faster and faster and lighting up with thunderous lightning.

Flashes of magic discharges shot up into the sky from the fort in the distance. Each flash brought a rumble to the ears of the men a few seconds later.

With a shriek, a shadow came through the blackened air and flew over the already darkened ground; the desdrak was back. It had not given up on catching its prey. It would not allow them to escape from its clutch.

A pillar of fire reached down, licking the ground by Rither and the others. The grass it hit was not set on fire; it was as if it could withstand the flames.

"Holy fuck!" Sizle cried, shielding his face from the heat. "That thing's going to kill us!"

Rither looked ahead. They were just a few hundreds leaps from the cliffs. They would have a natural shield against the desdrak. They were not there yet. They were far from it, and the giant beast might not miss its next attack.

Another burst of fire came. It burned its way through the arid air, turning it even more so. It made its way toward the men on the ground with nothing but a desire to kill.

Rynus held up his hand, and a blue wall of light materialized in the thin air. The flames crashed into it. Ripples, like waves, moved across the barrier from the point of impact. It became weaker, fainter.

The fire and barrier burst into nothingness. The desdrak shrieked in anger. It hadn't successfully killed its prey. They had gone unscathed from its fire for too long.

The demon soared through the sky quickly, placing itself ahead of its prey. It glared at them with blood-red eyes, and then opened its mouth to charge up more flames. A red dot appeared by its throat.

Rynus raised his hand again. A protective shield was put up, but the fire broke through. It was diverted and slammed into the ground beside them instead.

The young wizard sent up a ball of blue magic toward the desdrak. The Maenic was hit and sent tumbling through the sky, away from the men.

Rither led the others to the path leading through the cliffy area. The jagged rocks and cliffs quickly surrounded them. The desdrak couldn't kill them as easily, but they could not see where it was. They raced along the enclosed path.

The storm was becoming even more violent. Red thunder smote rocks, sending shards in all directions. From the center of the giant cloud in the sky, a twister of fire broke loose, reaching for the ground. A flock of black birds was engulfed. Rither heard their squawks of agony as they were sent into nothingness, only to be reborn just as they were.

Lightning struck a rock in front of Rither. The entire thing exploded, splinters flying in every direction. He was knocked off his feet, crashing into the others. The desdrak appeared in the sky above. It glared at its prey, visible now that a rock had been blown away, and charged up its fire.

A devlion lunged for the men, hunger dancing wild in its red-glowing eyes. It deemed the reward of getting the meal greater than the risk of trying to get it.

The flying desdrak let loose its magic. The flames engulfed the devlion. The hound fell to the ground, cooked to its very core. It had in a turn of ironic events saved the men.

Rynus quickly sent another blue orb at the desdrak. This time the Maenic avoided it, flying out of sight.

Rither got everyone on their feet, and urged them to continue running. They weren't far from the ruins—safety.

He looked up at the sky, scanning for the Maenic, but he could not see it; the desdrak was nowhere to be seen. Looking to his blades, disappearing behind a rock with a turn of the path, Rither took off after them, soon catching up.

They had come to a stop where they had first entered the giant field of rocks and cliffs, by the rock they had climbed up on and slid down from. They had to climb back up, and then a hundred leaps of open hillside led down to the ruined fort. There would be no shelter; they would be sitting ducks for the desdrak, unless Rynus's magic could shield them.

"This is it," Tryden said. "The home stretch, literally."

"Yeah," Emery agreed. "It ain't gonna be easy."

Sizle looked from Tryden to Emery to Rither. "But at least it's downhill, and it's not very far, so we'll probably make it. Right? Right!?"

Rither looked into Sizle's eyes. Should the young blade be killed, it would happen in moments, excruciating moments, but mere moments nonetheless. Telling him the truth would scare him without cause; knowing their chances would not help him.

Rither cleared his throat, meeting Sizle's eyes. "Of course we'll make it, Brother Sizle. We're guardian blades, toughest of the tough and bravest of the brave. No Maenic is superior to us."

Sizle nodded. He tried assuring himself what his master

said was true, but based on his countenance, it didn't work. Tryden looked calm, but kept glancing up at the sky, while Emery looked as frightened as always—not at all.

Rither looked to Rynus. His skin had turned paler and he was feverish. Using magic had sped up the progress of the affliction. Maybe when he spent his pool of magic energy on fighting the desdrak, he couldn't hold off the infection at the same time. Perhaps he was simply losing after a long battle. Either way, it looked like the end was nigh.

Tryden met his master's eyes. "Master Pleagau, I'd like to thank you for the past three years. After what happened to me, after... you know, you took me in; you saved me. It has been an honor serving under you."

"Same goes for me," Emery grunted.

Sizle looked from one to the next. Tryden was royalty, but could not return to his kingdom, Tryda. Why, Sizle did not know. He was not sure about Emery either. How had Rither saved him?

"It's been an honor serving with all of you, and, of course, especially you, Master Pleagau," Sizle stated. "You have not saved me, like you did these guys, but I appreciate the confidence you put in me."

Rither looked each of his blades into their eyes. He knew their chances were slim, but damn it, he would not give up; he would get all three back to Siva alive. They had sacrificed enough, more than most. They should not have to sacrifice their souls, as well.

"Let's do this," he said. "Let's make it back to our beloved home."

"So we can carve out Kritz's black heart," Emery said.

With one last look into the eyes of the others, the blades and the wizard turned to the rock and started climbing up. A hundred leaps stood between them and freedom. It would be over in a little more than ten seconds; in a few moments' time, they would be free, or they would be dead.

6

Rither led the others to the top of the big rock, and stopped to take in the view. A hillside led down to the fort that lay in ruins. A magical thunderstorm ravaged the fort and hillside, with a deafening sound.

With a shadow sweeping across the hillside and a shriek piercing the loudness of the storm, the desdrak announced its presence. It was like a hawk preying on squirrels; it was like a Maenic preying on humans.

"Run!" Rither commanded.

They took off down the hill. Every step closed the distance between them and survival, but for every second they spent on the hillside, they risked their lives and souls.

The desdrak swooped down toward them. Rither grabbed the sword on his back, readying himself to fight back.

The Beast Maenic came for him; it swept its long claws at him. His sword sliced at the hand. Two of the clawed fingers were cut off, but continued toward him, piercing his shoulder and sending searing pain through his body.

The desdrak shrieked, making the men fall to the ground in confusion, and then the beast flew up, away from them. Black blood was streaming out of its wounded hand.

The men rolled down the hill, slamming against the solid ground time and time again. Rither felt nauseated. His body throbbed. Every time he landed on his shoulder, the claws were pushed in deeper, causing him more pain.

When the hillside flattened out, they came to a stop. The world was spinning, and there were more than one of everything. Three of Tryden stumbled to his feet, shouting something, but Rither couldn't hear what.

"Master! Get up! The desdrak is coming back!"

One more firestorm came for them. Rynus raised a shield, and the fire slammed into it. With every drop running down his body, it was weakened. The fire had not broken through yet, but it was only a matter of time.

Rither used the light of the fire and magic shield to focus. Everything became one again; his vision became clear.

"Boss, get up!" Emery shouted.

Rither blinked rapidly. The desdrak kept up the fire, spitting it at Rynus's shield. He and the others were only twenty leaps from the ruined fort. They only needed to make it that last stretch.

Rither rose to his feet with Tryden's help. "Alright, let's go! Rynus, can you keep up the shield?"

"I don't know," Rynus admitted. "I can try."

"You can and you will. Our lives are in your hands."

They backed away from the desdrak, toward the fort. Step by step, they made it closer. The magical shield Rynus held up faded in color, while the desdrak kept up its fire steadily. The young wizard looked paler than ever; he looked as if he had no blood, like a corpse. His breathing had turned rapid, shallow, and labored.

The desdrak ceased its fire, and dove for them instead. It crashed into the magical shield, which broke up into pieces. The Maenic flew right through, continuing toward the men. The claws it had left were ready to carve through flesh.

Rynus threw a ball of magic at the desdrak. It crashed into it, exploding. The Maenic tumbled away through the air, but soon recovered its bearings.

"Run!" Rynus shouted.

They took off for the fort, the final ten leaps. The desdrak dove, much quicker than they could run. It had them right in its eyes. It would kill them and feed on their corpses.

The desdrak sped up the last few paces, getting ready for the kill. When they were but a leap away from safety, Rither spun around, swinging his sword at the creature. The blade slashed across its face, sending it wailing to one side and its blood to another.

Rither followed the others inside the fort. His eyes sought the portal. It was open, but no longer still and round; it was storming about, changing shape and intensifying and weakening intermittently. There was still time to make it back to Siva, back to Atae, back home.

"Let's go through the portal now, before it closes!" Emery shouted over the intensity of the storm.

Rynus shook his head. "No! Not yet!" They turned to him with questioning frowns. Why had he stopped them?

The room shook and rumbled as the desdrak crashed into the damaged wall. It was too large to fit through the hole. It shrieked at the men, charging up more fire. Rynus erected a shield of magic to stop the fire. It held strong, but weakened by the second. The desdrak's fire wasn't weakening.

"What is it, Rynus!?" Rither shouted.

"A thought hit me!" Rynus answered. "We've stopped the barrier from weakening further, but it is weaker than it was before! Even if we seal the gateway, the barrier might be too weak to hold strong."

"There's nothing we can do about that!"

The desdrak intensified the fire. The wizard grunted, and staggered to his knees. "There may be something I can do!"

"What!? What is it you can do!?"

Emery leaned in. "Boss, we ain't got time!"

Rynus closed his eyes and gritted his teeth, concentrating as much as he could. "I can repair the weak spot for good!"

"Why do I have a feeling it just isn't that simple!?" Tryden asked.

"It isn't!" Rynus said. "Immense magic forces—more than any one wizard could ever hope to wield—are required!"

"Then how the fuck will you do it!?" Emery wondered.

Rynus closed his eyes and looked away, while concentrating immensely to keep up the magic shield. "I must sacrifice my soul to feed power to the magic!"

Sizle's mouth fell open. "That's madness!"

"That's the only way!"

"I don't believe that!"

"I'm going to die, so I may as well do this! I'll make up for helping Kritz! I'll make up for... for killing my cousin!"

"What if your soul cannot find its way to Una from here!?" Tryden argued. "I'm guessing this kind of magic hasn't been used before, so what if your very soul is destroyed!? Dying is one thing, but losing your soul!"

The force field Rynus held up weakened even further, and he let out a cry of exhaustion. "What if the barrier is broken, and Siva is swallowed by Oblivion!?"

No one spoke. They all knew one man's soul wasn't worth the souls of everyone in the world. Rynus could restore the barrier, and he had to do it.

"I wish there was another way!" Rither told him.

Rynus turned away from the others fully, still concentrating on keeping up the shield. "As do I! Now, go! I'll close the portal behind you!"

Rither, Emery, Tryden, and Sizle backed from the wizard, toward the portal back to Siva. They stared at him, in awe of his sacrifice. The strain of keeping up the shield against the flames took its toll on Rynus even further. He sank closer to the ground in exhaustion.

With a scream, he rose to his feet, and an immense shock wave emanated from him, slamming into everything it came across. The men were pushed to the ground, the ruined fort shook, rocks came loose, dust filled the air, and the desdrak was thrown back, its onslaught of fire ceasing.

The portal destabilized further. Magic discharges shot out of it, smashing into the walls, roof, and ceiling. The desdrak clambered back onto the wall. Shrieking in anger, it threw another wall of fire at its prey.

Rynus screamed in anger, too, and another burst of forceful magic shot out from him. The fire was stopped in midair by the magic wall of air. The walls shook more. Larger rocks came loose, crashing to the ground. The floor split apart in several places, jagged pieces of it being pushed up.

Rither, Emery, and Tryden made their way to the portal. Sizle followed them slowly, staring in awe at the destruction. One of the pieces came up right below him, piercing his leg. He screamed in pain, and fell to the ground. The jagged rock broke off, still stuck in his leg.

Rither felt a stab of fear in his heart. "Anthony!"

He took off toward Sizle, running as quickly as he could. Jagged rocks shot out of the ground all around, threatening to pierce him just like one did Anthony Sizle.

Tryden looked back at the portal. It had settled in a state; it was not growing larger and smaller and intensifying and fading intermittently. It was slowly shrinking, becoming less and less.

"Master, the portal is closing!" he yelled. "Hurry, before it is too late!"

Rither lunged for Sizle, avoiding a piece of stone trying to impale him. He grabbed hold of the wounded blade brother. "Anthony, are you okay!?"

Sizle groaned, but couldn't speak; he was barely lucid. He grabbed hold of his master with surprising power, unknowing of what he was doing.

"I'll get you out of this," Rither said. "I'll save you."

He looked at Rynus and the desdrak. They were locked in a deadly battle of wills and fire. The world was crumbling all around them.

Rither threw Sizle over his shoulder. With one last glance at the wizard—the one who would save them all—he headed for the two other blades and the portal back to Siva.

Bright light came from behind him, but he dared not look back. The light was so strong that everything turned bright white; it was as if he walked through nothingness. Only he, Sizle, Tryden, and Emery had color. The dark portal was the complete opposite of the brightness all around.

"Boss, come on!" Emery shouted.

He and Tryden waved Rither in, urging him to speed up. The portal was shrinking more and more. It was not even a leap across, and it was constantly lessening. Soon, it would be no more than a memory.

Rither's legs throbbed. The claws rooted into his shoulder hurt, pain radiating through him. Lactic acid was building up in his legs and abdomen. There was not a particle of him that didn't hurt.

Sizle groaned, reminding him of the stakes. He didn't care about his own life or soul, but Sizle was worth fighting for. Emery and Tryden would never leave them behind, even if it meant their deaths. They were also worth fighting for.

The portal shrunk to little more than half a leap across. It was now or never; once the portal closed, there would be no going back to Siva.

The light became so strong he could not see anything; he was blindly pacing through the nothing. A beacon appeared to him, like darkness in the light; voices were calling out to him—familiar voices.

He felt a tingle in his stomach. Forever but for a moment, he and the others floated through time and space. They all became one with the fire.

7

Their feet touched the stone floor, and their knees buckled; they fell to the ground hard. Rither just lay there, clutching the cold, moist floor and letting damp air fill his lungs. The darkness that met his eyes was blinding, like light after one spent a long time in absolute darkness.

His vision returned; the scenery became clear. Emery and Tryden were lying a bit away from him. Sizle was lying next to him. He had his hand on the young blade's back.

He crawled to his feet. The ground wasn't just wet; it was covered in black blood, just as wet as when the Maenic had burst open. All that was left of the demon was where it had been before, but a path led through the blood.

Rither wiped some black blood from his face. He stared at it; he had not wrapped his head around what it was. Then it dawned on him, and in panic, he tried to wipe it all off, but soon gave up and looked to his blades instead.

He knelt down by each of them, checking their vital signs; all were alive, and Emery and Tryden were coming to. Rither let out a long and deep sigh of relief; he would never forgive himself if he survived and his blades didn't.

"Come on, get on your feet!" he shouted. Chaos still rang in his ears; he could barely hear himself.

With a groan, Tryden rolled to his back and stared at the darkness above. "You don't have to shout, Master Pleagau. I can hear you."

"What!?"

"I said that I can hear you."

The noisy ring in Rither's ears subsided. "Sorry, my ears were ringing."

"It's okay, sir."

Emery grunted, too, rising to his feet. "What the hell. My head is throbbing."

"Mine, too," Tryden said.

Rither did not speak. He just nodded, and looked to Sizle, who lay down, breathing but unconscious. The jagged stone stuck in his leg reminded Rither of his own pain. He pulled out the desdrak's claws from his shoulder, and let them fall to the ground.

"Maybe we should remove the rock," Emery said.

"No," Tryden disagreed. "If we remove the shard, he might hemorrhage; it might have cut through an artery, and is, as of now, stopping the bleeding."

Rither let out a heavy sigh, looking at the wounded blade. "Emery, could you carry him?"

Emery nodded once. "Sure thing, boss."

"We must find a way out," Tryden stated. "There were no branching paths the way Emery and I headed, and the way back and the way you and Sizle went are blocked off."

Rither followed the path through the blood with his eyes. It led to the passage he and Sizle had headed into. It was no longer blocked off; the boulders had been tossed aside.

Tryden stared at the opening to the corridor, too. "How... Who did that? Kritz?"

Rither watched Emery pick up Sizle with care. "He threw aside the rocks with his magic."

"Now ain't the time to discuss this," Emery said, carrying Sizle in his arms, rather than over his shoulder. The young blade looked so small. "I'd bet Kritz knows the way out."

"You are right. Tryden, draw your sword and stay close to Emery. I'm pretty sure both of you recall what's out there."

Both the other blades shuddered at the thought. Ancient ones hid in the shadows; they waited to kill those they came across; they waited to snuff out the flickers of life.

Rither led them through the sea of blood. He looked back at the wall with words. It was closed and he knew the portal had been closed for good because of Rynus; the weakness in the barrier between Oblivion and Siva had been repaired.

Only one task remained; they needed only do one thing to be finished with their most difficult mission yet; they needed to kill Angus Kritz.

8

Angus Kritz had left a clear trail of blood, his own and that of Od'kel. He had also left a trail of makeshift torches, made of tiny, magical fires burning on the walls. They followed the trail through the hallway Rither and Sizle had gone through before they entered the portal to Oblivion.

Rither led Emery and Tryden forth, the former still carrying Sizle. They had moved through the corridor for a while. Rither knew where they headed; he had been there before. It worried him, but not as much as going into Oblivion had.

"How's Sizle doing?" Tryden asked.

"The little runt is doing okay," Emery answered.

Rither took notice how for the second time since they met, Emery conveyed something other than calm, indifference, or anger through his voice.

"He'll be okay, Emery," Rither said.

"Yeah, I know."

"I don't think you do. But I promise you, he'll be okay."

"Are we sure the portal is closed, Master?" Tryden asked. "Do you think Rynus really closed it?"

"I am sure of it," Rither said, with a nod. "He mended the barrier, perhaps at the cost of his very soul; he untethered Oblivion and Siva, so a portal cannot be opened here."

The blades emerged onto a secluded ledge, overlooking a vast room, which reached up, down, and straight forward as far as they could see, but was merely a few leaps broad. The room consisted of several levels. Each level was a walkway lining the wall, which in turn was lined with prison cells.

Rither looked to the doorway he and Sizle had continued through. On their way back, they had run from the ancient ones, trying to fight them off. The unholy abominations were not so easily fought off; only by beheading them could they be killed.

He turned to the other way off of the ledge. A stairway led down to the prison complex. The trail of torches stopped, in the faint visibility of the vast room, but the blood continued down the stairs.

Rither guessed it was from there the ancient ones came. He guessed they had been prisoners of war, executed by the dragons and turned into undead warriors by potent magic; maybe it was the magic of a god—Drahc Uhr.

They had to go into the prison complex, where hundreds of ancient ones could be waiting for them. A couple of things made Rither not fear for his life as perhaps he should have, as he thought he would have.

The sense of dark magic—gravity—he sensed throughout the fort had lessened; it was but a fraction of what it used to be. He thought it was because the barrier was repaired, and most dark magic came from Oblivion. That which remained was the magic of the ancient ones.

The second thing that reassured him was that the ancient ones were mindless drones, with no intelligence; they were husks. Perhaps under the leadership of Maenics—dragons— had they been deadly and organized, but as it was now, the only thing they could do was swarm.

Rither took the first step onto the stairway, the others following him. They headed into what, quite possibly, was the vastest room they had ever seen. If not for the trail of blood left by the injured wizard, they wouldn't even have a remote chance at finding the way out of this cursed fort, if that was where Kritz indeed was heading.

They headed down the stairs, to a level lined with prison cells. Rither stared into the first cell he came across. It was empty; no ancient ones were there.

He looked across the room at the many cells, and then into the dark of the levels below. A faint thud turned his gaze to the other side of the level he was on. He saw nothing, but the sound had created a pit in his stomach, into which his heart fell. Glances from the others gave away that they also noticed it.

"Maybe it was a bird," Emery said.

Tryden laughed at Emery's awful attempt at a joke, which seemed to surprise even himself. "That seems plausible."

Rither smiled, but said nothing. Instead, he continued on ahead, carefully checking every prison cell he passed. They were all empty; no ancient ones were there. He saw the dirty floor and walls, the toilets overflowing with thick, brownish water, and the rotting mattresses on the floor.

The trail of blood left by Kritz continued past all of them, to a stairway made of wood. A small platform extended from the walkway, and the stairs led down from it, alongside the level to the one below. Rither stepped onto the stairway, but stopped when the step bulged and creaked. It did not break, so he took another step down.

"Walk carefully," he told the others. "The staircase might break."

They headed down, one step at a time. The wooden steps buckled and creaked, but held strong. When Rither stepped onto the platform at the bottom of the stairs and then to the stone walkway that made up the level he had descended to, he sighed in relief.

Soon, Tryden made it all the way down, as well, and both waited for Emery and Sizle. Together, the two weighed much more than Rither and Tryden did individually. Emery alone weighed the most of all four of them.

"Come on, Emery," Rither said. "One step at a time."

Emery took one careful step after the other, still carrying Sizle. The wood bulged so much it almost broke. He stepped onto the platform at the bottom of the stairway, and let the air in his lungs come out; he had held his breath.

"That was a close call," he said.

Rither smiled. "Yeah, it wa—"

The wooden platform broke, splintering downward. Emery threw Sizle to Tryden, who caught him, and grabbed hold of the side of the walkway.

"Help me up, maybe?" he asked.

Rither knelt down to help him, but halted. On the walkway on the other side, he saw a rotten human. Blinking, the human was gone; no one was there. Had someone, or something, been there or was his mind playing tricks on him?

Emery grunted. "Boss!"

Rither snapped out of his shock, and looked to Emery. He grabbed hold of his hand, and together, they pulled him up. Tryden handed Sizle to Emery, smiling to show appreciation that he was still alive.

Without another word, they turned to the blood-red trail and followed it with their gazes. It led to a prison cell a few leaps away. They headed to the cell.

The room was tiny; it was only four square leaps. Like the other cells, it was furnished with a broken toilet, which was flooded with dirty water, and a rotten mattress.

They stepped inside, examining the pool of blood that had amassed there; Angus Kritz had been there. Where had he gone thereafter? No trail of blood led away from there.

"Where'd he go?" Emery wondered aloud.

"I don't know," Rither said. "It's like he vanished."

"Do you smell that?" Tryden asked.

Emery sniffed, and then grunted. "I think it's the toilet."

"No, I think it is something else. It smells worse than the toilet would, even if the excrement has rotten a few hundred years."

"Whatever, bookworm, it ain't important. What matters is finding a way out."

Rither nodded. "Agreed. But where is that way?"

Tryden looked around the small room. "There has to be a hidden way out." He sniffed the air and frowned. "Seriously, you guys, don't you notice that?"

"I do notice it," Rither said, "but it's probably the toilet."

"Like I said," Emery stated.

Tryden drew his sword. "I don't think so."

"Emery, put down Sizle on the mattress, and let's look for the hidden way out," Rither said. "If there is one, that is."

119

Emery did as he was told, carefully placing down Sizle on the mattress. He looked at the little man, tilting his head to the side with fondness. His mouth twitched, seeing the leg; a shard of rock was pierced through it, and blood had made the torn leather armor wet and red.

"Alright," he said. "Let's look."

Stale air breezed toward them. They looked at each other wonderingly. How did the breeze come to be in the enclosed prison complex?

"Out of the way!" Tryden shouted, pushing Emery aside.

From the dark outside the cell, a human came for them. Its pasty skin stuck too close to the bone, and the eyes were white and dead. It wore a red piece of cloth around its neck down to its knees, covering the middle of the body, but not the sides. The cloth was tied in place around the waist with a belt. This was just a husk of a human.

The ancient one threw itself at Tryden, but instead, it hit his sword. It slid farther down the weapon to the hilt. Its eye had been pierced, but it was still alive, and tried to reach for him with its arms.

He pulled the sword to the side, splitting open the head. The ancient one staggered back, out of the cell and into the railing of the walkway outside. The monster tumbled over it, into the darkness below.

Tryden glared at Rither and Emery. "I told you something smelled bad!"

Emery drew his sword. "Fine, you were right. Do you always gotta make a big deal of it?"

Rither drew his sword, too. "I should've listened to you." He leaned out of the cell to see what was happening. Dozens upon dozens of ancient ones were coming from both sides. "Brother Tryden, you look for the secret path. Emery and I will hold them off."

"Yes, Master Pleagau," Tryden said, facing the cell's back wall to look for any signs of a hidden path.

Rither turned to Emery. "Remember, sever their heads."

Emery cocked his head to the side. "I know, boss."

The ancient ones came for them, bringing with them the

wall of stench, like flies around dung. The dead eyes locked on to the men. The lipless mouths were clenched tight.

Rither swung his sword to the side, beheading two of the ancient ones. Emery swung his sword, too, killing two more. Four were far from all; dozens swarmed to the cell, trying to squeeze in to kill.

Emery charged ahead, his sword pointing forward. Half a dozen ancient ones were impaled on the sharp weapon, and he pushed them back, showcasing his inhuman strength.

"Close the cell door, boss," he struggled to say.

One of the creatures could match him, physically, and he held back six on his sword and more alongside them. Rither guessed he could do so only because they were surprised, if undead monsters could be surprised. Either way, he would not be able to hold them back indefinitely; they would push back, sooner or later.

Rither moved forward, swiping his sword sideways, severing the heads of many of the ancient ones. He then pulled at the barred gate, trying to slide it shut, but it was stuck.

"Emery, we need your strength," he panted. "Switch!"

Emery screamed and dragged his sword to the side, completely splitting open the ancient ones stuck on the weapon and slicing into the ones standing nearby. He swung about his sword, ending many of the ancient ones.

He threw his sword to the side, and launched himself at the barred gate, while Rither swung his sword in an arc at the ancient ones now trying to get in.

Tryden scanned the wall for clues as to what happened to Kritz, but the dark made it hard. He feared magic was needed to get out; he feared a disguised transportal needed to be unlocked before being used.

Screaming, Emery yanked loose the cell door. It slid shut with a squeak and clang, slamming into the other side and locking automatically.

He picked up his sword. "I sure hope this is the way out, boss"—he glanced at the ancient ones bending the bars—"or else we're fucked."

"I don't see anything, Master Pleagau!" Tryden shouted.

Rither glanced at him. "Keep looking! It has to be here!"

Emery stabbed the undead. The bars were set too close to each other for him to swing his sword, so decapitating them was difficult. He had to stab them repeatedly, turning their heads to a paste, before their bodies fell to the ground.

Light, which Rither could only call dark light, shimmered from above. As opposed to darkness, it illuminated the area and made it visible, but unlike light, it was dark. It was like it didn't care about the laws of nature; it existed to fight the rules established by the Gods or by nothing to be there because a world cannot exist without rules to govern it.

Everyone stopped what they were doing; the ancient ones ceased their attacks, looking up at the light instead, and so did the three conscious men. At the center of the dark light, Rither saw the silhouette of a man. It looked similar to the ancient ones, but more majestic.

Its skin was also pasty and wrinkled, but did not stick as close to the bone. Its face was only remotely human. Rather than being shaped like a normal head, spikes made of bone and skin stuck up, forming what looked like a crown on the top of its head.

Its eyes were not white and dead; they were black, with a pupil of white. They scanned the blades in the cell actively. Rither thought they looked alive, but at the same time, they were definitely dead.

The creature wore black robes with blood-red linings, and a cloak fluttered in a nonexistent breeze, as if the garments were held by a gust of dark magic. Perhaps it was that same gust that kept the creature suspended in the air.

The creature hissed, showing its teeth filed into triangles, as sharp as knives. Rither felt like he understood it; it spoke no words, but he knew it wasn't merely a mindless beast. It was undead, but it wasn't dead. It was something completely different, a new class of enemy.

Whatever it was, it hissed once again, but this time at the ancient ones. The undead soldiers started bending apart the bars of the cell door, as if they were listening to the majestic one above them; it commanded them.

The blades still could do nothing but stare, and continued to do so as it reached up its arms, holding them wide apart. A mist of energy made of the same dark light as surrounded the being materialized between its hands, beams of the dark light shooting out from it in all directions.

"Tryden," Rither said slowly.

Tryden gawked at the creature. "Yeah?"

Rither shook his head, tearing his attention from the undead creature. He grabbed hold of Tryden, and shook him. "We must find the way out!"

Tryden blinked in surprise, meeting Rither's eyes. "Yes! Of course! Sorry, Master!"

He turned to the back wall again. He saw only dust: dust, dust, dust, blood, dust, dust. He shook his head.

"Blood!" he called out. "I see blood here!"

"Where?" Rither asked, glancing at the majestic creature, which was still charging up its magic.

"Here," Tryden said, pressing his hand against one of the square rocks that made up the back wall.

The rock slid inward as he pushed his hand to it. Then, a second later, the entire wall came loose, like a door on hinges. He pushed it open, revealing a narrow cave path beyond and letting in a puff of cold air.

"Let's go!" Rither shouted. "Emery, grab Sizle!"

Emery threw Sizle over his shoulder, and he and Tryden headed into the hidden tunnel. Rither looked to the creature suspended in the air, charging up the dark light between its scrawny, dead hands.

Their eyes connected, and it felt like they stared into each other's very souls. He saw nothing but darkness in its heart, which didn't even beat anymore. While many undead beasts had been made evil by magic, but could have good, corrupted souls, that was not the case with this one; its soul was a dark void.

Rither forced himself to look away. The monster let loose its magic, hurling the fog of dark light to the cell. Rither fled into the concealed path and closed the doorway behind him. As he sprinted to the other guardian blades, a forceful blast followed him, and then words echoed through his mind.

"The end is nigh, mortals," the voice hissed. "Oulpas—the Seventh Bone Priest—has awoken."

9

A light was shimmering up ahead. It was the most beautiful thing Rither had ever seen. He imagined that it looked like Sivana's holy smile, Her divine face. He had never laid eyes on anything more mesmerizing.

He, Emery, and Tryden stumbled into the light, and then toppled over in exhaustion, falling to the soft grass beyond. He just lay there, filling his lungs with breath after breath of fresh air. Nothing had ever felt so good—nothing at all.

The sun had recently risen. Rither didn't realize how long they were in there; for hours, they had chased Kritz, clashed against Maenics, and saved the world. No one would know; they were knights of the Guardian Blades, unknown heroes stalking the enemies of light from the shadows.

He pulled his hand through his beard and up through his hair. Perhaps it was time to shave, he thought. Rising to his feet, he looked to the cavern from which they just came. No ancient ones had followed, but he couldn't get the voice out of his head.

What the voice said troubled him; if it were true, it would mean the worst was not yet behind them. It stated Oulpas— the Seventh Bone Priest—had woken up. It seemed true; the special ancient one was the Bone Priest.

Multiple pieces fell in place, all at once—the Machine, the seven keys to power it, and the seven Bone Priests.

The Wall of Stories at the Temple of the Precursors was vague about what the Machine was or did, but according to legend, it was some sort of weapon, built by Adolle Hite—the First Bone Priest—and his six followers. They cut off a finger each to make the skeleton keys and sacrificed themselves to feed power to their creations. For their devotion, Drahc Uhr gave them eternal life; He made them Bone Priests.

Rither had always thought it was but a story. Sure, it was common knowledge, and many believed it, even though no one knew exactly what the Machine was or did, but Rither still thought it was just of legend.

The only thing he knew for sure was that Adolle Hite and his six followers were the ones that summoned dragon eggs into Siva; they instigated the Dragon War, which nearly laid waste to mortal life; they were the vanguard of evil.

Rither focused on something else; he looked at the trail of blood on the ground, following it with his eyes and taking in the scenery at the same time.

They were in a shallow forest. Behind them, cliffs covered in vegetation led upward toward Fort Lockdown, which was visible in the distance. They had been beneath the cliffs all along, beneath this beauty. Tapron trees—small leaf trees—surrounded them. Their leaves were a mix of green, red, and yellow, a beautiful display of the many shades of life.

"Come on," Rither told the others. "On your feet. We need to catch Kritz."

Emery rose to his feet, helped Tryden up, and then picked up Sizle. "We need to find him, so I can carve out his heart with Cutter, my long-trusted guardian. I will feed his soul to the nearest pack of wolves."

Tryden nodded. "Agreed."

They trailed the blood through the flora. Rither could not get over how good it felt; the sun felt comfortably hot, even though summer was coming to a close and fall was around the corner. He could not recollect ever seeing such a beautiful late-summer day.

A cool breeze caressed his body and hair. It also filled his lungs with freshness, breathing new life into him. It tasted sweet in comparison to the stale air he had breathed in the fort; it didn't stink of decay.

Gazing up at the sun, he thanked the Precursors for being alive, and to cover all his bases, he thanked the Divines, too. All of them were gods, worthy of his worship.

His eyes fell on something less pleasant than the beauty of the tapron-tree forest; Kritz had fallen and dragged himself leaps across the flat grassland that cultivated the forest. A thick blood trail showed where he had collapsed and how far he had dragged himself.

He was still alive, and smiled when he saw the blades. He was pale, though; he wasn't long for this world. "Ah, so you made it out. Well, almost all of you. I apologize for running. It is... not something I take pride in."

Staggering to his feet, he stumbled toward Emery. "Let me make it up to you. I can heal your wounded soldier."

"Do you think I'd let you touch him!?" Rither growled. "Do you think I am that dumb!?"

Kritz shook his head. "I'm not trying to fool you; nor am I trying to help you. I want to restore my pride, something the Maenic lord, Drahc Uhr, deems highly important."

"He's not wrong about that," Tryden said.

"Look, either you let me help him, or he dies; it is simple as that. His entire leg has been chewed through. As soon as you remove the shard, he will bleed to death. If you wait too long, he'll lose the leg. I'm the only wizard within tileaps. I'm the only one who can help him."

Rither nodded, but refused to look the wizard in the eyes. "Brother Emery, place Brother Sizle on the ground."

With a look to Rither, which wasn't returned, and a hateful look to Kritz, which was returned, Emery placed Sizle on the soft grass. "You better not hurt him."

Kritz sneered at Emery, but then gave Sizle his undivided attention. He put his hands on the young blade. An aura of light surrounded them. The shard of stone was pulled out of Sizle by an invisible force. Blood flooded out, but after less than a moment, the bleeding stopped; the wound started to heal. Moments later, it was gone completely.

"Get back!" Rither ordered Kritz, who did as he was told.

The blades knelt down by Sizle. Rither felt his pulse, his strong pulse. And then the young blade opened his eyes. He looked from Rither to Tryden to Emery, where his stare settled. The large man was smiling at him.

Looking at the blue sky, Sizle put a wide grin on his face. "Hey guys. Is this Evengarden?"

Tryden smiled and shook his head. "No, Anthony, you are in Siva. If this were Evengarden, do you not think the Gods would have fixed Emery's ugly mug?"

"Yeah, and they would've sewn shut your wide mouth, so you ain't gonna bother us with no more of your trivial shit," Emery retorted with a faint grin.

Rither faced toward Kritz. "Thank you for saving him. But why didn't you save yourself?"

Kritz grunted, pressing his hand against the wound in his gut. "I cannot." He looked to Emery with hate. "Your soldier caused too much damage."

Rither nodded. "It serves you right. Now, we made a deal, remember? Tell us about the two with whom the war starts, and tell us what we can do."

Kritz clenched his jaw, and gritted his teeth. "You already know much about the other plan that's been set in motion. It has to do with the Machine and the Winds of Change."

"The Winds of Change?"

"The skeleton keys, as most know them."

"Ah. And what is it the Machine does?"

"You know that. I won't waste my breath telling you."

Rither nodded once, keeping a hateful stare at the wizard. "Then tell us what we don't know."

"Oh, but there is so much you don't know," Kritz stated, a smug grin on his face. "As I said when we first met... In fact, it was not the first time I met you, Master Blade." He turned to Emery, and smiled a wicked smile at him. "It was not the first time we met, either."

Rither looked at Emery. He could tell that the large man was nearing his boiling point. He turned to Kritz again. "Get to your point!"

"My point is you know so little, yet think you know much. There is nothing you can do to win this war, but I'll indulge your thirst for hope."

"Then tell us!"

"The next battle in this never-ending war will begin with two people, as I've already mentioned. They are the one who is reborn as Drakhi and William Bishop. These two sides of a coin will clash, deciding the fate of the world. Drakhi is on the side of good—Maenics. He will save us from the tyranny of chaos with which the false gods rule us."

"So he'll build the Machine?"

"Yes. He is very close to being finished, very close indeed; he needs only one thing, and he knows where to find it."

It annoyed Rither how Kritz was sneaking around the answers. "What is this thing? And where is it?"

Kritz signaled with his hand for Rither to come close. The blade master glanced at the others, before doing as the wizard requested. The wizard whispered in his ear.

When Kritz was done, Rither moved back. "You may have him now, Emery."

Emery neared Kritz. "Ten years ago, you raided a village, my village. You... killed my little girl. And you took my wife. What did you do to her?"

Sizle looked up at Emery with wide eyes. "The tale Master Pleagau told us was about you!?"

Kritz smiled, but blood came up instead. "They were your wife and daughter, huh? Your daughter really was cute."

"My wife! What did you do to her!?"

"I used your wife for something more special than a mere faerhart; I used her to bring Krava to this world."

"Krava!?" Tryden wondered. "He is a wizard—a man! He's been working with the Black Hand for years."

Emery stabbed his sword into Kritz's leg, making him cry out in agony. "Don't fucking lie to me!"

As Emery pulled out the sword, Kritz wrapped his hands around the wound. "I-I'm not lying. He is not human; he's a Maenic. He's my greatest achievement. He would've been my second greatest one, had you traitors not come here."

"You sacrificed my wife to bring that piece of shit into the world!? You disgust me! You ain't nothing but filth!"

Kritz glared at Emery with his black and white eyes. "And you disgust me, dog."

With a grotesque smirk, Emery closed in on Angus Kritz. His face and the immense pain he caused were the last two stimuli the wizard experienced. Then his soul was sent right back to Oblivion, where it belonged.

Emery breathed heavily. He was covered in Kritz's blood, from head to toe. He held Kritz heart in his hand, and as he squeezed, he said, "That felt good."

Tryden looked Emery up and down, and turned to Rither without commenting. "Master, what did Kritz say to you?"

Rither looked into Tryden's eyes, and then also Sizle's and Emery's. All had the gleam of curiosity. "There is work to be done. We must travel to the Kayan Isles, posthaste."

Rither turned from his guardian blades and led them into the wilderness. Warmth washed over them, and after saying a couple Thalmanian words, they vanished.

With a thud, Sizle walked into Emery. "Sorry."

"Watch it, brother runt," Emery grunted.

"Crazy first mission, huh?" Tryden asked with a laugh.

"Yeah," Sizle answered with a nervous chuckle. "I hope we won't have to do that again."

"Really!?" Emery wondered. "I thought it was pretty fun!"

"Of course you would think this was fun," Tryden said.

Rither did not join in the discussion. He grinned, listening to the others and taking in the calm of the Cyran forest.

Shielded by a cloak of invisibility, the four knights of the Guardian Blades of Siva strode into the battlefield, ready for their next encounter; they were ready to save the world from the imminent next threat from Oblivion.

Night had settled upon the Dragonlands, like a shroud of darkness wrapping itself over everything and everyone, and the light of dawn was far away.

The Long Lost Tales of the Dragonlands

The Winds of Change

***

Patrick Hall

On the following pages, you will find a brief excerpt from Patrick Hall's debut novel, *The Winds of Change*, due for publication on December 9, 2013. It is the very first novel in the *Dragon Hunter series* of *The Long Lost Tales of the Dragonlands* franchise, whereas the trilogy you just read—the first in the *Guardian Blades series*—serves as something of a prologue.

This isn't necessarily a representation of the final product, but a preview of what to expect. Nothing is written in stone, and changes from this version may be present in the finalized product.

This is a work of fiction. All the characters, places, creatures, events, and contents of the book are either a product of the author's imagination or are used fictitiously, and any resemblance to any persons, living or dead, business establishments, events, or locales is entirely coincidental.

ISBN-13 (The Winds of Change paperback): 978-1491278772

Prologue, part one
Prophecy

In the dead of the cold night, rain pounded against the house on the hill. Wind swooshed by and lightning struck down, casting a short-lived, but eerie light on the area.

The still room was lit up only by a lonely candle, standing on a small table against which a man was leaning, snoring softly. The messy room was scarcely visible in the weak candlelight, but one could still see the outlines of all books that lay open, papers that were strewn about carelessly, and half-eaten fruit that had been chucked to the floor, some covered in a fine mat of mold.

All was evidence of an obsession for knowledge. The man had read the books for several years, searching for what he wanted—needed. He didn't yet have the knowledge he sought and chances were he never would.

Something tapped softly on the window. It was barely audible over the louder pounding of raindrops, but was certainly there. It snapped the snoring man from his deep slumber. He opened his eyes, and scanned the room for what had awoken him. He heard the soft tap, and, wondering what it was, got up and gazed to the window. It was too dark to see anything. Slowly, he headed for it, with a tight grip of his warmth.

A sudden flash of lightning illumined the outside. A jolt of fear ran through him when he saw a silhouette outside in the rain by the window, mutely gazing in without moving a muscle. The light faded to darkness, but he could sense the figure and feel its gaze upon him. It was unnerving, to say the least.

He decided that standing around would do no good. Warily, he continued to the window and opened it. A powerful gust stormed inside, bringing leaves and water with it. The silhouette stood in the downpour, silent and waiting.

"Who are you?" the man demanded to know.

"Who I am is of no consequence," the silhouette answered.

"Answer who you are or I'll burn you to cinders. It wouldn't be the first time I've done such a thing. You'd do well to believe me."

"I believe you could, my lord. I am Til of the Old People."

The man backed away from the dark shape—this alleged man of myth. "That can't be! You cannot be an elder!"

"It be so, my lord. You'd do well to believe me. We've business tonight. Don't worry; it will not take much of your time."

The two stared at each other. The man fell to his knees. "I am deeply humbled to be in the presence of an elder!"

Til looked annoyed by his gesture. "Wizard, get up!"

The man—wizard as he'd been called—glanced up at Til with a wide-open mouth. He shut it, and rose to his feet. "What is it the Old People want with me, a mere gifted one?"

"It's been six years, Wizard. Is it not time to let go?"

The wizard let out a heavy sigh. "I can't." A hint of a tear came to his eye. "I just can't."

"I didn't expect anything else. There's still something you need to do, Wizard."

"What?"

"You'll stay in this wretched, lonely place another seven years. There is nothing I can do about it; mages always were stubborn. However, in the year three hundred forty-two, you'll hear of three events. The first is the death of a king— Fendon Alamain."

The man's eyes grew wide, and his mouth fell open. "You have predicted Fendon's death?"

"The next is the printing of a book—The Winds of Change."

The sorcerer's eyes grew wider. "The Winds of Change? I could swear I recognize that phrase."

"Perhaps you do. The third is the birth of Drakhi."

This time, the wizard's eyes became normal and he closed his mouth. "Drakhi? Who or what is Drakhi?"

"What, I cannot say, because I do not know. To whom this one refers will become clear in time."

"Why not just tell me?" the sorcerer grunted.

"The time has not yet come. You will know in seven years. All you need to know is he will be a threat to Siva, our existence. Do you know what the Machine is?"

The wizard nodded. "Yes, of course."

"Do you know what it does?"

The sorcerer quieted down. "No. No one does."

Til sighed. "If only it were so. There are people, bad ones, who know what the Machine is, does, and how to use it. I don't know who they are, but I do know the Machine will be used by the one I call Drakhi."

"Do *you* know what it does?" The wizard's usually gentle voice was on the edge of irritation. "Or can you not tell me that?"

Til sought the gifted one's eyes. "It breaks the barrier between Siva and Oblivion. It'll bring the fires of destruction to Siva."

The wizard's eyes widened more than ever, and his mouth fell open again. "That's impossible! Is it not?"

"Let me tell you something about immortal history few realize. It is believed when the Precursors and Divines raised the barrier, the Maenics tried to push it back. It is because of this we cannot communicate with the Gods; the barrier separates all of us, all of the three planes of existence. Now for what few know. Because it was pushed back and spread thin, the barrier isn't impenetrable. It can be broken, not from Oblivion or Evengarden, but from the mortal side. The Gods have magic to destroy it, if They were here in Siva. This is where the Machine comes into play."

"So the Machine has the power of gods?" the wizard wondered, astounded by the knowledge. "Tell me what I must do!"

Til shook his head. "There's nothing you can do now; you'd

135

be killed. I'd like for you not to remain in this house the next seven years, but we both know you will anyway. Seven years from now, there will be something for you to do. There is a prophecy, which speaks of the one who can defeat Drakhi. Two sides of a coin will clash, one for Maenics, the other for mortals and the Gods. Only one can succeed; only one will. Drakhi's one. The other, the hero of all, is someone you know. He will need help if he is to succeed; you must collect his heirlooms. You know which ones."

When Til said that he knew which heirlooms, the wizard's face lit up, with unbridled hope and desperation and an undertone of irritation. "Who is it!? Who is it I know!? Please just tell me!"

Til met his eyes. "The hero of all is one William Bishop."

As the gifted one blinked in surprise, Til of the Old People vanished into the storm, into the night, into the darkness.

Prologue, part two
Emancipation

It was late in the afternoon. The sun remained high and proud in the light-blue sky, glaring at William Bishop—a boy on the verge of manhood. But it was now steadily going down in the north.

William's thick-but-soft, brown hair was sticking to his sweaty skin, and to see anything with his green-blue eyes with a ring of golden brown around the pupil, he had to squint. The blistering heat was almost too much to stand during daytime, but he preferred it much to the numbing cold of night. Somehow, the sand beneath his feet found its way inside his shoes.

But now was the time to pay mind to neither. From the safety of the viewing balconies surrounding the sandy arena, hundreds of eyes were glowering at him. The eyes belonged to blurred faces William couldn't and didn't care to remember; they were featureless faces that would haunt him for an eternity.

Also down in the sand was a man, twice the size of William; he must have been two leaps tall. Clad in only the finest steel there was and armed with a sword sharper than the tooth of a dragon, he was a fearsome opponent.

William had rusty iron armor, barely holding together over his raggedy clothes, and a dingy iron shield and a worn-out sword. It was a miracle his equipment hadn't crumbled into dust.

The large man dashed forth, and the screams of the crowd followed, cheering for blood. William reacted to his enemy's assault by diving to the left, dodging death by an instant.

The crowd fell silent; excitement was in the air.

The large man swung his sword at William, who ducked in the nick of time. He swung his sword, but was countered by another attack. The sheer power threw him in one direction and his blade in another. His sword arm was painful and sore. The brute stood over him, and raised the glimmering sword to finish the job.

William thought of what he was told before the fight: "This one last battle, and you will be a free man or a dead man." There was no way he'd die when he was this close.

He kicked his opponent in the leg. The big man fell over by the hard kick. William rolled to the side, and dashed like a madman to the rusty sword in the sand a few leaps away. He seized it and turned around just in time to parry a blow with his shield, which was abolished by the sheer force. He swung the blade, to his own despair as it bounced off the man's armor with a clang.

Fear spread through William, like poison. If he could not even harm his opponent, how could he ever hope to make it out of the arena alive? And the crowd didn't care; as long as someone died, they didn't care.

William felt a fist in the face, forcing him down to the ground. His opponent approached him, slowly, and the blade came down. William rolled aside. He got on his feet, and saw that his foe was trying to free the sword from the sand. He took a firm hold of his own weapon. As hard, but precise as he could manage, he thrust the blade at the man's face, into the slit of the visor allowing him to see. Blood stained the sword and flowed onto the sand.

All was silent. Then, as the bulky man tipped over and hit the floor, the crowd exploded with cheers. Hundreds of persons were saluting William, because he had taken another life he shouldn't have needed to take.

But at least he had his freedom.

***

William was a free man now; he was no longer a slave. What was he going to do? He had nowhere to go, no one to go to.

"Still better than being a slave," he muttered, as he walked out of the arena and into the Bloodhalls, the rooms and halls where combatants and owners would prepare for battle beforehand and clean up if victory was achieved. The bodies of the less fortunate were dragged through the halls to be disposed of. The stains and streaks of blood left by the loser gave the halls their name.

The room was made entirely out of stone, and sported just two colors—gray, and red. The weapon racks, mannequins, benches, and—through an archway to a separate area—primitive showers, made of wooden tanks with dirty water and valves, were the only things in the room.

He approached the weapon racks and mannequins, on which he put his rusty sword and armor. The gear wasn't his, but that of his now former owner, who'd be furious and hunt him down if he took it. It did not matter how old and useless the things were; they were not his and Alfred Stonehart had gone to great lengths to tell him this.

William was deep in thought when someone started speaking. "Hey, boy! I'm talking to you!"

He turned from the mannequin he'd placed the armor on, and faced the man. "Yes, sir?"

Alfred Stonehart was huge—three times the width of a normal man, though not any taller. He had a stuffed-up, round face with a neat mustache he took much pride in. He wore a tan shirt and pants, a fashionable cloak around his wide shoulders, and boots made of woohl skin—a rare commodity.

How many men had perished acquiring the woohl skin? Alfred Stonehart truly deserved the family name passed on to him; his heart really was made of stone. Compared to William, though, he looked like royalty. A fat and ugly king, but a king nonetheless.

Stonehart put a threatening finger on him. "Just 'cause I don't own you anymore does not mean you can stop giving me respect, you piece of shit."

"No, sir. Of course not, sir," William said with as much respect as he could muster, hiding his rage as best he could and forcing himself to hold back the punch he desperately wanted to give his former owner.

"And you owe me a shield."

"Excuse me." A third man entered the room. "William is a free man, as per our agreement. He's got an equal claim to be treated with respect as you do. Isn't that right?" The tone of his voice let Stonehart know he should not try to argue.

The man stood in the open doorway behind the slave owner. It was hard to make out what he looked like, as the bright sun had nearly set behind him. William could make out, from his outline, that he wore a cape and had a sword sheathed in his scabbard, hanging in his belt.

Alfred Stonehart took hold of William's arm, placed something in his hand, and let out an angry snort. He walked out from the room, but when he got to the man, only gently squeezed past, as if he were afraid. William thought it looked funny when a man of such generous proportions tried to squeeze past another without disturbing him.

But at the same time, Alfred Stonehart looked smaller than he usually did. He was scared out of his mind of the unknown man, and that worried William greatly. Alfred Stonehart usually didn't fear anyone; he was to be feared. Who could command so much respect, from Stonehart no less?

The unknown man approached William. As he came closer, he became distinguishable. He had on the finest armor William had ever seen, from head to toe; it was all white, and lined with gold. The sword had a white and golden handle, and its scabbard, too, was white and gold.

The man removed his helmet, and kept it under his right arm. His brown hair swirled to his shoulders. His gray eyes stared at William. They felt penetrating, as if they could gaze into his soul. "Hello, William. I am Sir Ryan Anderson."

Sir Ryan Anderson. He was a royal knight, who had sworn an oath to protect the innocent and vanquish evil wherever possible. No higher honor could befall a man than being named.

He gave William a kind look, with his piercing, gray eyes. "I've seen you battle, and must say, you are quite resourceful, though you may not be the strongest or fastest... yet."

William's heart leapt so high it almost came out of his mouth. "Are you going to name me a knight, sir?"

Ryan Anderson laughed, and smiled warmly. "You're much too young and inexperienced," he said, to William's great discontent. "Nor do I have the authority. Perhaps in time, you will be named; you do show promise."

He took a gentle hold of William's arm, and led him out of the depressing, bloodstained room. William was ashamed to walk in his tattered clothes next to the elegant knight.

The only item of value he owned was a necklace his father had given him. The necklace was barely of any value, but attached to it was what his father had said was a dragon's tooth. He couldn't know if it was true; not many believed in dragons any longer. If it were true, it would be worth a lot of coin.

He looked at the trinket in his hand, and then hung it around his neck, where it was supposed to be.

The dirt street reeked of sweat and blood, and was filled to the brim with people, most much filthier than William. An absence of people took shape around the knight. Surely, they weren't fearful of the noble knight? Unless they had reasons to fear such men—especially those carrying swords and wearing armor as strikingly beautiful as it was powerful.

For the first time in years, William felt a sense of security and happiness. He could not help but grin, as Sir Ryan Anderson led him through the crowd, toward a new life.

***

After a half hour of being hauled through the masses, the harbor came into view. It was equally full of crates as it was with people. The stench was instead one of seaweed and enticing spices, with only a gentle undertone of the stench that plagued the rest of the town. Grand ships were anchored by the waterfront.

Ryan pushed their way through the crowd. When they reached the grandest ship William had ever seen, they stopped. Anderson let him take in the sight of it in silence.

An Imperial flag—a white background and fifty gold stars, one for each nation of the Empire—fluttered from one of two masts. A Cyran flag—a black background with a triangle of white reaching from each of the bottom corners to the above center, with a black silhouette of a knight stabbing a dragon in the triangle—fluttered from the other.

The knight sought William's eyes. "Now, you've got a choice to make," he said, his tone serious, but kind and friendly. "You can come with me on this ship and I will take you to Solitude, where you will train with the Royal Order of Custodian Knights at Skyward Palace, or—"

"Yes! I'll do that!" William said in excitement.

Ryan smiled. "Or I can take you home to the Summerset Isles, where your parents' farm is waiting. You're nearly an adult."

William was dumbstruck, not because he didn't know what he wanted, but because he had not thought of his parents in a long time—not since it happened.

The knight seemed to understand, as he put a caring hand

on his shoulder. "It must be hard. I'm sorry."

"No, it isn't." It was a lie. "I'm fine. I want to be a knight, sir."

Sir Ryan Anderson studied his face thoroughly. "Very well, I'll take you to Solitude, where I will train you personally. It won't be easy. It'll take years. Today will surely be the day your childhood dies." Yet again, he scanned William. He sighed, and added, "But I have a feeling it did that a long time ago."

TO BE CONTINUED

IN

THE WINDS OF CHANGE,

DUE FOR PUBLICATION

ON

DECEMBER 9, 2013.

About the author

Even as a little boy, Swedish author Patrick Hall had an interest in writing. It's been a lifelong passion of his to write, but to do so professionally didn't enter his mind until January 2012, when he started writing his debut novel, *The Winds of Change*. That book is the pinnacle of his short life, and a realization of his dreams.

Now that he is grown up, writing seems like the only logical thing for him; it's the one thing he can see himself doing for the rest of his life. And he's just gotten started. The Winds of Change is his first novel, but it shall not be his last.

Thank you so much for reading, and stay tuned!
The journey is not yet over...

www.authorpatrickhall.com
www.facebook.com/patrickhallofficial
www.twitter.com/AuthorPatHall
patrickhallofficial@gmail.com

With the warmest regards,
Author Patrick Hall

Patrick Hall, author of
The Long Lost Tales of the Dragonlands.

Made in United States
Troutdale, OR
04/25/2024

19433829R00098